Praise for
The Brooklyn Leprechaun
Mystery Series

(The Brooklyn Leprechaun is)
"Delightful—full of fun, humor, action and adventure"

Penny Warner, National Bestselling Author,
'How to Host a Killer Party!'

"Brooklyn Leprechaun is a great Celtic romp—I want a Mick of my very own!"

Suzanne Johnson, Author
'Royal Street and River Road'

"If you are a young adult or young at heart, this is a mystery to entertain and inspire".

Dorothy Churchill, Author
'From Mourning to Morning'

"The Brooklyn Leprechaun Trilogy captivates the reader by expertly combining history, magic, romance and suspense. A total delight for all ages."

Sally Smith, Author
'Am I My Brother's Keeper?'

Book One
The Brooklyn Leprechaun
Takes place in Ireland and introduces Bridget to her Fae family.

Book Two
Royal Spirits
Takes place in England and helps Bridget build courage and confidence.

Book Three
Magical Scotland
Takes place in Edinburgh and Iona, Scotland as well as Ireland. Bridget lets go of the past and her fears as she helps the Fae take on Morrigan.

Magical Scotland

By *Bernadette Crepeau*

Magical Scotland
Book three of *The Brooklyn Leprechaun mystery series*
All Rights Reserved.
Copyright © 2011 Bernadette Crepeau
Library of Congress Control Number: 2011900952

ISBN 10 146818508X
ISBN 13 9781468185089

PRINTED IN THE UNITED STATES OF AMERICA

Acknowledgements

Writing is a team effort. Thank you dear friends, without your help and continued encouragement this book would not have been possible.

I would especially like to thank Lynne Borden. Your patience with me is amazing, thank you so much for your friendship and support.

I also wish to thank, Susan Bushman, Kearin Duarte, LauraJane Kendall, Judy Simons and Sally Smith.

Dedication

Thanks to our ancestors we have been given a great opportunity to enjoy life. Please don't let your dreams die. You are never too old to see them become a reality.

Cast of Characters
& Places

Aunt Molly
Bridget's aunt from Dublin, Ireland, who is now a fulltime House Brownie.

Bridget
Born in Brooklyn, N.Y, she inherited land in Ireland where she met her immortal ancestors. She is street smart, but lacks confidence. The Fae people have, what they call, a few minor challenges to build up her courage before she must take down Morrigan, and save the entire Fae race. Her faeire and leprechaun blood helps, but first she must believe in herself and allow her powers to come.

Charlie Boyle
Detective Inspector assigned to the Criminal Investigation Department at the New Scotland Yard.

Cathcaruth
A holding place for Fae under Morrigan's influence.

Dagda
Appears as a corporate executive except for the sickle of death he carries. He is Morrigan's second in command.

Cast of Characters
& Places

Dorgis
Some of the Queen's Corgis were mated with dachshunds
 to produce a new breed called, Dorgis.

Fergus
Fergus is a Dryad. A tree spirit who is well connected with
Mother Earth.

Friar Xavier
Friar Francis Xavier is a five hundred year old spirit who
watches over the royal family.

Geraldine
Faeire, Queen of all Fae, cousin to Morrigan, and Bridget's
many times removed great-grandmother.

Iona
Actual place and wonderful history, most of which is
correct as mentioned. I did elaborate on the number of
buildings at the Abbey; and descriptions are my
imagination at work.

Mary
Bridget was raised by Mary's mother since the age of twelve
and considers Mary her sister.

Cast of Characters
& Places

Michelle
Born and raised in France. Veterinary assistant for the Queen's prized dogs.

Mick aka Lord Howth
A handsome wizard, who must shift into the guise of a Brittany spaniel to mentor Bridget in all things magical.

Morrigan- Goddess of War
She wants Fae power to assist her in worldwide destruction. To accomplish this she needs to take over land in Ireland and all of the Fae. At present she only has control of the Elder Fae, some evil Fae and creatures she has created.

Niamh
A teenage faeire warrior and trainer.

Padraig
Is King of the Leprechauns, husband to Queen Geraldine, and Bridget's many times removed great-grandfather.

Peter Carins
Bridget's gifted cousin whom she hoped would move to Ireland, take care of the land, and keep it safe for her Fae family.

Cast of Characters
& Places

Que-tip
A teenage faeire from England.

Sandringham Palace
20,000 acre home to the royal family.

Simon
British secret agent and Mary's boyfriend.

Skeletor
Is the name given to a spirit that appeared on a CCTV camera at Hampton Court Palace, October, 2003.

Stan...
Afghanistan

Tristan
A teenage leprechaun warrior and trainer.

The Wedding Cake
Queen Mum's Memorial is nicknamed *The Wedding Cake* as it represents the decoration on the top of one.

♣ x ♣

All is Possible!

First Believe

Then Achieve

INTERLUDE

Morrigan Watches

 *Morrigan opens a portal and watches future events unfold hundreds of miles away.*

The bright, sun filled day suddenly darkens. Diffused light seeps through the canopy of trees. A non-human cry is heard as a tree falls, hitting her bike. Blood gushes down her face and over the rocks. A shadow emerges from the woods. A fierce wind removes any trace of her passing.

In a clearing stands a man. He admires the liquid dripping from a sickle he holds in his hand.

Morrigan gleefully moves her black snake staff to close the portal.

"You thought a mere mortal could outwit me. You will soon be in tears my cousin when you see what the future holds for the Fae without their prophesied heroine."

There is a Celtic saying that heaven and earth are only
three feet apart, but in the thin places
that distance is even smaller.

CHAPTER 1

A Thin Place
Iona, Scotland

"RECALCULATING, RECALCULATING!"

"Alright already, that does it." I continue arguing with the GPS as I park the Mini-Cooper on the side of the dirt road. "It's not here! This island's only three miles long and is only one mile wide. We've been over it a dozen times. It's *just not here."*

I look around, and all I see are green fields and rocks. Thousands and thousands of rocks, with no house or tree in sight, it's got to be here somewhere. This is the place Mick said the training camp was. Dang it, where is it?

Okay, I'm losing it. I'm arguing with a machine. Maybe I need to walk around a bit. Perhaps I can see the house from that hill over there. I cross the dirt road and climb, what I first think of as a grassy knoll, but, as I continue to climb, I pass a sign that says it's *Dun Hill*, the highest point on the Island. Yikes no wonder I'm getting tired.

The scenery's unbelievable. To the East I can see *The Abbey*, the pride of the island of Iona. Further East I can just make out the ferry landing.

A wall of fog covers some of the buildings on the waterfront and is heading this way. Great it's almost sunset and now fog. The Scottish landscape is rugged and beautiful. It's as if I've stepped back in time. Way back. I wouldn't be surprised to see dinosaurs walking across the rocky plains.

This part of Scotland may be part of the British Isles, but so different from Ireland and England. *Forgetabout* Brooklyn. We have no places like this back home. Okay, I give up. It's getting late. I'll go back to the village and ask for better directions. Why did I trust a talking dog anyway? I turn to climb back down the hill, stop and stare.

My little rental with the annoying GPS is now parked on a drive in the middle of a forest. Rising above the tallest trees I've ever seen is the top of a castle. Never one with a loss for words, my jaw drops open, and I'm speechless as I take in the medieval view.

The castle towers several stories above a large, high-walled garden. It's probably built of pale stone, but sunset's fire turned it gold and gilded the roofs and chimneys. The same magic washes over the surrounding evergreens.

Green, yellow, pink and purple flags wave in the breeze. Watchtowers are at each corner manned by sentries. The walls must be at least 16 feet high. The garden or commons area between the wall and the castle itself must be a mile wide and two miles long.

What on earth? Where did this all come from? Wait a minute. Am I actually questioning a castle appearing out of thin air? I've met my ancestors, 'The Immortal *Greats*,' and I'm being tutored by a talking dog, so what's a castle appearing where there once were only rocks. As my Aunt Molly would say, 'It tis a fine place to be learning magic.'

I follow the long driveway through the forest and drive over a moat to the sound of bubbling water. The walls of the stone archway leading to a circular drive show off mosaics made of the pink and green stones, I noticed on the beach.

As I enter the common area the sentries blow their horns, and the commons fills with dozens of Fae folk, many with wings spread as they appear, all smiling and welcoming. It looks as if a rainbow exploded. I start to laugh and no longer feel tired.

I park in front of a massive door that's opened by Aunt Molly. She's looking younger each day. She doesn't look like a senior citizen at all. Here among the Fae, she looks in her thirties. Maybe it's her bright, multicolored housedress decorated with animals, lime green apron, and bright pink sneakers. She looks like a walking advertisement for a zoo. I'm glad she's taking my fashion advice. Hmm, I wonder if my faeire and leprechaun blood will help me look young when I'm her age.

"Come in! Come in, a thousand welcomes." Molly exclaims as she heads to the car to help with my bags. After a quick hug, and a wave of her hand to transport my bags to my room, Molly says, "How was the ferry crossing? You must be starving. Let's get you settled in."

A young imp rushes over. "I am so sorry my lady, you see the louts put me up to it. They said that if you were the rightful one from the prophecy, than you would see the castle right away. I should have had it appear sooner."

Aunt Molly puts her arm around the girl and says, "Bridget may I introduce you to Harmony. She is our gatekeeper. Her role is to produce a cottage for all to see and interact with any visitors. I am certain she has learned her lesson and will not be listening to that gang of hooligans ever again."

"Never again, I promise." Harmony says as she glares at a few leprechauns standing off to the side, looking everywhere but directly at me.

"No problem Harmony, I'm sure I would have seen the castle right away if I had not let myself get so stressed. It was the minutes I took to enjoy the scenery that allowed my gifts to surface."

"Come along then, all is well." Molly says as she leads the way into the castle.

I'm glad she doesn't see my mouth hang open again as I take in the ancient castle. I thought Buckingham Palace was a work of art. This one is just as beautiful and feels even older. The entrance is a rectangle room beneath a high vaulted, gilded ceiling. The room's elegance is highlighted by the dull gleam of lacquer that had surely coated the incredible furniture for centuries. It is complete with all the castle trimmings one would expect: tapestries, veined-marble museum quality statues, and even a suit of armor stands guard.

The stone steps lead up about thirty feet to a landing that branches off in two directions. The colors are spectacular. I feel as if I'm in the clouds. The white marble entranceway is accessorized with various shades of blues.

I follow Molly, making myself relax enough to appreciate the objects d'art I'm passing and try to remember the route. We take a long hallway on the right and walk past several doors. Molly then opens a door to a room four times the size of my studio apartment in Brooklyn. The sixteen foot high ceilings make the large, wood, canopy bed seem normal size. There is even a massive dresser, vanity, and a walk-in closet with enough space for a small clothing store.

"Wow, this is ..."

Molly smiles and points to a door, "Your washroom is right through that door. I filled it with my own special fragrance but if you prefer..."

"It's perfect. Thank you so much." I run to my aunt and hug her. "You're the greatest."

"Wash up now me girl, I'll get us some tea."

After getting lost in the huge hallways, I open another massive wood door to a cathedral size room with tables set to feed fifty. Dazed, I follow the sound of Molly singing and find a kitchen, but not the medieval one I was expecting. This kitchen is right off HGTV with stainless steel appliances and all of the latest gadgets. Molly comes over, takes my arm and leads me to a chair.

"You must be starving. Sit yourself down. I have tea all set."

"Food's a great idea, where's Mick?"

"He had to step out for a moment, should be back shortly."

"Great, I can't wait to see him again. It's only been a couple of days and, can you believe it, I miss him."

"How was the ride over on the ferry?"

"Fantastic, I'm glad you reserved a rental car for me. It's scary that they only have one car to rent out."

"The rental will be returned by one of the boys. That way it will be available for others. This island is a national treasure. The local government only allows six vehicles on the island at one time. That way they can control pollution and unwanted visitors," she says with a smile. "You know the tourist that only complains about what we don't have, rather than appreciates what we do have."

I nod and smile in agreement. I can't stop looking around. "Molly, this place is fantastic. How many people live here?"

"I am happy you like it. It can be a bit much and takes some getting used to. Right now, we have many folks living here, but it can sleep over two hundred."

She continues to wave her hand, and the cozy little table is soon loaded down with tea and sandwiches.

"So you had a little trouble finding the place?" Molly smiles as she pours tea for both of us, and puts a generous amount of honey in her cup.

"You could say that. First there are no trees at all. Now I'm in a forest. A wee bit of magic is my guess."

"Ah, now, we don't want just anyone dropping by."

I sip my tea and look at my Aunt, the first magical family member I met. I was stunned when Aunt Molly told me that my ancestors, or who I refer to as my Greats, asked her what she desired as a gift for helping to save the Fae land. She has always had a wee bit of Fae magic, so she asked to be taught how to use it fully. She is now a full time *House Brownie*. Which is great, I love having magical folks in my life.

Well some of them. There are those who are pure evil and some who don't want to do terrible things but are under Morrigan's influence. They are made to do things against their will, which is horrible, and one thing I hope to stop.

I look over at Molly. It seems as if I've known my aunt all my life, and yet it has only been a few, very busy months.

Molly looks at me, puts her cup down and asks, "A penny for your thoughts dear."

"I was just thinking of how much has happened since Mary and I left Brooklyn for a *short* two week vacation," I laugh. "Let's see, we saved the Fae land from its mortal enemies, caught a murderer and terrorist. Even found a cousin in England and stopped St. Paul's from being blown to pieces. Now Mary is dating a British spy, and I'm to be trained in magic so that I can stop the Goddess of War from taking over the rest of the Fae, and the land that's my ancestral home."

I look at Molly and smile, "Hmm, I wonder if this is what folks call a working vacation?"

Molly laughs and shakes her head.

"Rumor has it that you had a grand time in England. You met the Queen of England herself and danced with a Lord?"

Molly's eyes are shinning so I'm sure she heard all the details. My first chance to meet a Lord and it has to be the guy who picked me up off the floor at the reception, after a waiter knocked into me.

"Oh, how embarrassing, not the Queen, she was great but did the rumor say *how* I met the most handsome Lord in the entire world?"

"Hmm, something about this handsome Lord helped you up from the floor, and there you are wearing a lobster in place of a hat?"

Molly laughs and I join in not that I'm over being embarrassed about the lobster incident it's just that Molly's laughter is so contagious.

INTERLUDE

Fae Kingdom
Mayo, Ireland

Padraig ran his hand back through his blue black hair, his ever present smile missing as he asks, "My Lord Howth, how is the training progressing? Our Queen is fading fast, and the threat of Morrigan's followers grows daily."

"Bridget's time in England has given her a tremendous amount of confidence. I believe she is ready to tackle serious training. She has arrived safely in Iona. We will begin immediately."

Not liking the look of fear in his friend's eyes, Mick places his hand on Padraig's arm.

"Dear Friend, weren't you the one who told me that all will be as prophesized and, that I needed to relax?"

"I need not remind you that the Fae depend on the queen personally. It has been the practice since time immemorial. Our queen protects the people, the lands she holds, and the businesses she administers. Her strength fades with each Fae put under Morrigan's controls. She can no longer take mortal form and soon her immortal form will be non-existent. Mick, my friend, our survival, depends on that wee girl."

"Ensure our queen that I have faith Bridget will succeed. Ask her to hold on a few more weeks and we will be ready."

Mick, a handsome, immortal wizard, shifts from his human exterior into the guise of Bridget's mentor and his Brittany spaniel form.

CHAPTER 2

Meet the Trainers
Iona, Scotland

"Sounds like a party in here, what am I missing?" Mick asks as he walks into the room, his paws making a funny clicking sound on the slate tile floor.

"Nothing much, just telling Molly about my time in London."

"You look a little tired Bridget. Perhaps you need an early supper and a good night's rest before we begin training."

"I'm okay. I would like to meet the trainers or protectors you were telling me about."

"Tristan. Niamh. Appear!"

A faeire warrior, about my age appears, wearing a silver mini-skirt, colorful leggings and a white Afro. Next to her stands a leprechaun warrior who looks about three or four years younger than me. He's like fifteen or sixteen. Both are at least a foot taller than Molly and even taller than me. He's wearing worn out jeans, green T-shirt, red and gold sneakers. He winks and smiles at me before he turns to Mick.

"Grand. Now, please introduce yourselves to Bridget."

The boy bows his head to me, "I am called Tristan, and I have fought beside Nuadha, the King of the Tuatha de Danann. I am to be your protector."

"Hah, you mean your father fought beside Nuadha."

"Now Niamh, don't be spoiling a good story with the truth."

Tristan grins at Niamh, with mischief and love in his eyes. Niamh pushes his arm and she announces in a clear, strong voice.

"I am Niamh. I am to be your protector. My family is a member of the Tuatha de Danann."

"I'm very pleased to meet you both. I turn to Niamh and tell her, "You remind me of a friend I had in England, her name is Que-tip."

Tristan laughs so hard he falls to the floor. He looks at the hateful look from Niamh and laughs harder.

"Que-tip is a cousin of mine." Niamh turns her back to the laughing Tristan and continues, "According to the latest tale, it would seem that a long lost relative has been found. She alone has the power to release us from Morrigan and return our Queen to full immortal life.

"We also heard stories of someone who can send Morrigan followers to the holding place. Now *that* is interesting. It is the first time we have heard that story."

"Heck, you even sound like Que-tip. Yeah, I can handle Morrigan followers," I look down, not particularly pleased with my gift.

"I'm not happy about sending Morrigan followers to the holding place or ending the life of Morrigan's creatures, but I guess if that is what I have to do to help my Fae family, then I will do it the best I can."

A more serious Tristan speaks up, "Not that most of her followers have any choice. Morrigan's spell hits all

Fae folk above the age of centaurea. Then we are compelled to spread the disease of hatred and ill will. We will lose control of our bodies and minds, as our parents have. We must stop her soon."

I look at the young warrior. He looks like he wants to cry but is holding back.

"It is hard to believe that one woman is doing all of this."

"She is an evil deity that grows stronger with each human war. She is no longer alone. We have received word that Morrigan has Dagda as her second in command. He is a powerful creature. Dagda is known throughout the land for his cruelty and greed." Mick announces.

Molly looks at all of our sad faces. "Time enough for this kind of talk later. Why don't you all take a drive to the Abbey while I finish dinner?"

"Grand idea Molly. Niamh, please drive."

I look over as the strong, dignified Niamh holds her hands out to Tristan for the keys.

Tristan makes a face at her, and she sticks out her tongue.

Wow, if these two are my protectors, I'm in trouble.

CHAPTER 3

The Abbey
Iona, Scotland

"Wow Mick. This place is amazing. It's twice the size of some of the villages I've been in. What can you tell me about it?

"In 563 AD when St. Columba and his followers came here from Ireland they founded a small monastery made of wood, wattle and daub. Later, the timber was replaced with stone, and around 1200, the Columban Monastery was transformed into a Benedictine Abbey. Numerous additions were made to the building from then until the mid 16th Century. The architecture of the church has been determined by the demands of its monastic community, local congregation and pilgrims, so its shape evolved to meet their needs."

"It doesn't look as though it was built that long ago. It's in remarkable shape."

"It is treasured by the Island inhabitants."

The Abbey is the size of a small town. I walk around the outside and look at this incredible building.

"Wow look at these."

"Those tall, intricately carved preaching crosses date from the 8th and 9th centuries."

"This is beautiful. Too bad more people don't know about it. I would hate to see it neglected like many of the ruins I have visited. This is living history."

Mick points to a small hill surrounded by an ornate fence, *"All that remains of the monastery is the enclosed bank that defined the holy site, and Tòrr an Aba, 'Hill of the Abbot', where Columba is believed to have died in 597."*

"What's that building?"

"That little stone building is called St. Columba's Shrine. Next to it is a door leading into the Abbey church. Many believe that it may date from the 9th century. By then, Columba's monastery was subject to repeated Viking raids, and late in that century the saint's relics were taken for safekeeping to Dunkeld in Perthshire, and Kells in Ireland. The famous Book of Kells, now on display in Dublin, was probably made on Iona."

We walk around for about an hour, and I'm beginning to drag. Mick looks at me and says, *"I am sure that Molly has dinner all set, let us return to the castle."*

We pile back into the car. I sit in the back next to Mick. Niamh is driving, and Tristan looks as if he's pouting.

"You said that this castle is owned by my Greats, do they come here often?"

"Not since the troubles have escalated with Morrigan. It is now necessary for the King and Queen to stay in Mayo, to protect the land."

INTERLUDE

Mary Plans a Surprise Visit
London, England

"Simon I must do this, I seriously need to speak with Bridget. She's my best friend and she needs to hear our fabulous news in person."

Mary holds her hand to the sunlight streaming in from the floor to ceiling windows. She admires her ring for the tenth time since she entered the room.

"I can't tell her on the phone. She said in her letter that the place where she is staying has no phone service. Her cell won't even work. She can't hear it from someone else. She'll be devastated."

"I understand that, but it will take time to get there. That is not a short hop on a plane as it is to Ireland. You need to write to Bridget and let her know you are coming, fly into Glasgow and then take a bus to the ferry.

"Then, when you are on the island, you will need to rent a car. Good Luck with that. I have heard stories of people walking miles to see the Abbey because there were no cars or bikes to rent.

"I hate for you to go on your own. Can you not wait until my duty in Wales is finished?"

"I want to surprise her. Don't worry, I have a few days off work now that our product has shipped, and you'll be busy in Wales."

"It'll take two days to get there. If you are certain, I'll write down the directions."

"You've got to be kidding me. Where is she in Outer Mongolia?"

"I warned you; first you have to fly from London to Glasgow, Scotland. Then take a bus to the train station. From Glasgow you go to the seaside town of Oban which takes about three hours. There you need to get a room for the night. Early the next morning you take a ferry from Oban to Craignure on the Isle of Mull, another hour or so. Then there is the bus travel across Mull to the village of Fionnphort, about an hour depending on how many sheep the bus encounters on the road. And finally, there is the ferry from Fionnphort to Iona."

"I only have a week!"

"The journey will take you through some of the most beautiful countryside in Scotland but will take you two days to get there and two days to return. I wish you would wait until I can travel with you. Remember that I will be out of mobile range. We will be unable to communicate via our mobiles or the web, what if anything goes wrong?"

"Don't worry. I will be okay. I only plan to be gone a week. I will meet you back at your flat a week from today. I promise."

CHAPTER 4

Training Begins
Iona, Scotland

Early the next morning I meet up with Mick, Niamh and Tristan in the kitchen garden.

"First I wish to show you how to concentrate and make a sword appear."

I look at Mick as if he's crazy, but after a few attempts, I learn to hold my hand out and visualize what it is that I want to appear. First I get a knife to appear. Everyone laughs, but I'm real proud of my knife. Mick insists that I concentrate and change it to a sword. I concentrate, and it changes to a cutlass that is too heavy for me to hold, and I drop it. I try again. First I look at the sword Niamh holds and then I create one just like it for myself.

Everyone applauds and a couple of the Elves dance around. Everyone is smiling. Then Mick asks Niamh and Tristan to demonstrate the basics of dueling for me. Wow, I'm not an athletic person and he expects me to accomplish dueling? I watch Tristan and Niamh while Mick is explaining their footing, posture, moves and strategies. Finally a time-out is called so we can take a break and eat the hardy breakfast Molly has prepared for us. Then we return to the garden for long hours of practice. Eventually Mick has me sparring with the other two. I might not be polished and smooth in my movements but I'm getting the gist of it. Is it my imagination or is some of my Fae heritage kicking in. I'm actually handling this sword like I have a clue what I'm doing!

After a few days of dueling practice, Mick takes me aside. *"Bridget, now we try something a little different."*

Mick levitates a canister out the kitchen window and holds it in mid-air.

"You've got to be kidding?"

"You can do it. Concentrate."

"Okay, I'll try the bigger one."

I concentrate on a large canister. It lifts off the shelf, floats to the window. Just before it leaves the building it explodes. Kaboom! Flour covers every surface in Molly's kitchen. Mick drops his canister to the ground. He and I run into the woods.

"I guess I should try a smaller one next time. What happened?"

"Your power of concentration is strong. Lighten up a little."

"Okay, I'll try."

We stop running and look around.

"I love these trees, aren't they beautiful."

I hug an ancient white oak tree then collapse on the ground beneath its leaves and rest my head back on its trunk. Mick lies down next to me and puts his head on my lap and asks, *"What are you thinking?"*

"I read something a while ago that felt right, felt important, but I never knew why."

"Do you know why now?"

"I think I do. The article said that, you gain strength, courage, and confidence with every experience in which you stop to look fear in the face. You must do the thing you think you cannot do."

"That is excellent advice. Who is the author?"

"Eleanor Roosevelt. She was the wife of one of our presidents. She's right. I'm frightened, but I can't give up. I have to help my family."

"Family is important."

"I've never had a family before. I guess being a member of a family takes some effort. I mean, we can't just take them for granted. We need to do everything we can to help them when they need it, right?"

Mick is silent, but even with my eyes closed I can tell he's looking at me. I guess after the adventures we've been through we've gotten really close.

"Bridget, if you could have anything in the world, what would it be?"

"Peace. I don't want the Fae to fear war or have their home taken from them. How will they survive without all of this beauty around them?"

Mick closes his eyes. He can feel her pain. He looks at her bowed head, steps forward and begins to transform to human shape. He reaches for Bridget to comfort her, stops and shakes his head.

He returns to dog form, and says, *"Can you climb a tree?"*

I open my eyes and just look at Mick, his voice sounds weird.

"Bridget?"

"Are you serious? Climb a tree? I never got much chance to do that in Brooklyn."

Mick looks at me and teleports me to the limb of the tree above us. "What...? Help!"

Bridget, please open your eyes. Look around and enjoy the experience..."

I open my eyes, look down to the ground and see Mick looking up at me. I'm about thirty feet up on the lowest limb. I scream and hold on for dear life!

"This isn't so bad, but the limb could still break! How do I get down from here?"

"Don't always be in a rush, enjoy the moment. Look out over the top of the trees. See how tall and majestic they are."

He pauses. *"Look there, to your right, see the deer?"*

I look at hundreds of trees in various shades of green. I see the deer gather at the edge of the field and listen to a large variety of birds.

"It's so beautiful here. It will be hard to go back to Brooklyn."

"Every place has its own beauty, we only have to stop and look."

"You're right. I don't stop to look around very often. I'm usually rushing from one place to another. How would the Fae survive if they did not have this incredible land?"

"The trees and deer have many challenges, yet they survive. With every challenge, we grow stronger. Your family will be okay. You will too."

"I hope you're right."

"What is your life like in Brooklyn?"

"It's okay. I work for a temp agency. Going to a variety of jobs is fun. The work is okay, but it's hard to make friends. Where we live... is okay I guess. I never had much to compare it to. You get used to everything and sort of except it as normal, know what I mean?"

Mick nods.

"We do know all of our neighbors. That helps to keep us and our things safe. Knowing your neighbors is rare in the city."

"Why are you so sad?"

"I know why you're keeping me up here, so I'm not frightened of flying. You want me to do incredible things to help my family. But I don't feel magical. I'm not like you. What if I can't help them?"

"Look around Bridget, the one that created all this created you. You can do anything you make up your mind to do."

I look around and look down at Mick.

"You're wise for a dog, aren't you? Okay, bring me down."

"Bring yourself down. Concentrate on what you want to have happen."

I look at Mick, smile, and close my eyes. I concentrate. Mick yelps as I transport him next to me on the limb.

"Ah, you're so cute, you yelped like a little puppy. I thought you were used to the flying thing."

Mick does not look happy. Hmm, is he glaring at me?

"It was the surprise of it. Dogs do not climb trees. I see that you have mastered the art of levitation."

"I can't say I mastered it. I can't get down."

Mick appears on the ground.

"Of course you can get down. Concentrate on what you want to have happen."

I close my eyes and materialize on top of Mick. We roll around the ground. I can't stop laughing, I jump up, and run, Mick chases, I hide, and Mick materializes next to me. I don't know when I ever played like this.

After awhile, Mick and I sit in the sunshine. I pick a few dandelions. Mick lies next to me. I would like to stay here forever. I wish the horrors of war would go away and leave my family alone.

Mick nudges my arm and I pet his head. "Can you tell me more about Queen Geraldine?"

"What do you want to know?"

"Why's she almost transparent? She was always a little translucent but now I have to struggle to see her."

"As with a human mother, her children are a part of her. With the loss of each Fae, a part of Geraldine ceases to exist, she fades."

"What was Geraldine like before this began?"

"Our Queen was a terror to anyone who dared to hurt the British Isles. She would become mortal and take on the guise of powerful women. She had many names, some you may still find mention of in your history books. In Ireland, she was Grace O'Malley a pirate queen. She would take back goods stolen from the people, and return it to them. Many Irish looked to her for protection, many businessmen wished her dead.

"In Scotland, she had many favorites, Isabelle of England in 1285. She was the wife of Edward II of England. She took up arms against her husband and his

supporters. When Edward III came to the throne, he forced Isabelle to flee to Scotland, where, during the ensuing war, she travelled with a defending troop of like-spirited women including two sisters of Nigel and Robert Bruce.

"Then there was the mortal form of Isobel, Countess of Buchan. In 1296 Isobel MacDuff left her husband, the Earl of Buchan. She made sure to take the finest warhorses with her, to fight for the Bruce. A cause for which her husband did not approve, the earl went as far as to issue a warrant for her death. Then there is the mythical Queen Scathach of Skye who trained the hero CúChulainn."

"What changed?"

"Morrigan became jealous of her cousin. Our Queen is loved by all and was extremely happy. She was also growing in power from Mother Earth and the happiness of the Fae."

"Morrigan's powerful but I doubt if someone that evil would be loved or happy. If the Queen of the Fae can't stop her, how on earth will I?"

"Bridget, we will put a stop to Morrigan. She will not win."

I stand. "You're right. Life's here and now. And now we have a kitchen to clean."

We run back to the castle and come to a halt when we are met at the door by a scowling Molly covered in white flour.

Molly holds a broom in one hand and a dustpan in the other. Silently she hands me the broom and ties the dustpan to Mick's tail.

The elves in the garden roll on the ground laughing.

CHAPTER 5

Training Continues
Iona, Scotland

Every day is the same, up at dawn and train. Break for a meal, then train some more. When the weather is bad we train indoors, I did find that landing on slate flooring is much harder than landing on grass, but I'm getting the hang of this flying thing. Mick grins like a proud parent when I do well. It's been over a week, and I want to go back to Ireland, but Mick hesitates, he wants me to keep training.

We're all taking a break and eating in the large dining room when I ask for the hundredth time, "When are we going back to Ireland?"

"You, my impatient friend, have much to learn. Have you read the book I gave you?"

"The Clan of Scotland?"

"Yes, do you understand how crucial the Clan Chiefs were to the people?"

"I believe so. It seems that the Clan leader provided everything for his people. He made sure they were fed, housed and safe. Without him for protection the Scottish way of life may not have survived."

"Indeed. In a similar fashion many countries depend on their leader. The Scottish Clan System is much the

same as the Fae. It has been the system since time immemorial. The Fae are dependent on the Queen personally, not only for the lands she has protected. Their entire way of life is in her hands, a precious way of life that is now threatened."

"If Morrigan isn't stopped, if I fail they won't lose just the land. They will lose the very thing that makes them who they are… Fae power."

"Correct. Fae power has stood at the heart of Fae life for centuries untold; it is a spider's web of connections and support that links everyone who shares their blood. Fae power is the very essence of their life; without it, they will die. Again similar to humans, people respect and depend on their leaders. If a leader looses that respect, people lose all trust and hope."

"The power that helps Geraldine is the land. The land I inherited. I was able to stop a mortal from taking it. Now I must stop Morrigan. If she takes over the land, then all is lost. I've learned enough. We must return and help them now."

"Soon."

Later that night I try to sleep. I look around my lavish bedroom. I wonder why I can't sleep.

After all of the training exercise I usually fall asleep quickly. Maybe I need white noise. I smile in the dark. Mrs. G. liked what she called white noise. She would play a classical radio station or hum while we were studying.

When I think of Mary's mom, Mrs. Gallagher, I always smile. I was never allowed to call her by her first name, only mom or Mrs. G.

Mom never came easily. I thought the use of that word a special gift that only Mary had a right to use. Somehow I had been denied the privilege of a mom of my own. I wonder what my life would have been like if my mom hadn't died when I was born.

Well then I wouldn't have had Mary in my life. The day we moved into the building...

The memories come so fast I can't stop them.

It had snowed that day. As I carried our belongings to our new apartment, I remember that I stuck my tongue out to catch the snowflakes and marveled at how the city could look so clean and pretty under a layer of snow.

That night Dad was angry. He had to pay the landlord his whole paycheck and not enough was left over to buy more beer. He was yelling and when he came towards me, I knew I was in for another beating. I ran downstairs, and he followed me. I opened the vestibule door and ran outside. He slammed the door shut. I was locked out.

There I was sitting on the cold stone steps and wishing it was summer. I could have rung one of the other apartment doorbells, but I didn't know anyone, and, if I had rung the super's bell we would have been kicked out for sure.

When I heard people coming I hid behind the garbage cans and waited, the only noise was my teeth chattering and the rats scurrying in the garbage.

A couple of hours later a man came up the steps. He used his key to open the door. I ran as fast as I could to catch the door before it shut.

I knew I could get into the apartment because I'd hidden a key earlier. I knew what I would see when I opened the door. Dad was passed out on the bed; I covered him with a blanket. I had looked at the clock, wrapped dad's coat around me and sat in the chair to sleep for a couple of hours before I had to be at my new school.

In the morning I was a little late getting to Sister Mary Francis's third grade class and she was very upset.

She had made me stand in front of the class as an example of the sin of slovenly appearance. My white uniform shirt was not ironed and my hair was not brushed enough.

Sister Francis had grabbed my hair and a pair of scissors. She was going to cut my hair off as a lesson to the other girls in the class. Mary had jumped up from her seat and had begged Sister on my behalf. She had promised Sister Francis that I would look better the next day and I did.

That afternoon she took me home to her mom. I was so happy to find that Mary lived in the same building as I did.

I never had to tell Mrs. G. that we didn't own an iron or hairbrush. From then on we never gave the Sister a reason to think I was slovenly.

I hear Mick's paws gently scraping on the door. "Come in Mick, I'm not asleep yet."

Mick jumps on the bed and lies his head down on my hand.

"What are you contemplating Bridget?"

"Oh, I'm just remembering when I first met Mary. I know you said several times that we cannot relive one second of the past, that sad memories drain us, but this is a sad memory mixed with a happy one.

"I understand. Memories like that help you keep in touch with the past. They remind you of who you are and where you came from and what you need to be."

"The major reason I'm sad is for all of the people who believe they are trapped in a situation like I was. People who have given up hope and see no future. They believe that living with pain and fear is normal."

I smile as I look around my castle bedroom.

"Not that this is normal." I hug Mick and he licks a tear off my cheek.

"But everyone has a right to go to sleep at night pain free, and without fear of the future. If only I could give them the gift of our ancestors, the strength and courage to look at their lives and make positive changes. Not only make a better life for them but to ensure that there will be a better life for future generations."

"One way to ensure that is to be the best you can be, and that starts with a good night's sleep."

"Stay with me Mick, I'll go to sleep, I promise. But somehow having you next to me helps to keep all the bad memories away."

CHAPTER 6

Peter & Michelle
Iona, Scotland

"Mick, I have to do something. My cousin Peter just delivered a letter from the law firm that owns the apartment, our apartment! This is horrible news! My friends and neighbors are being kicked out of their homes."

"Peter and Michelle's home?" asks a puzzled Mick.

"No, in Brooklyn, the guy who owns my old apartment has a contract with the Olympic committee, and they are tearing down my old neighborhood to build the new site for the summer Olympics."

"Your cousin Peter is okay? Perhaps you had better sit down and slow your speech somewhat so that I can make sense out of what you are saying," Mick suggests.

I sit down and take a deep breath.

"When I was in England, I emailed the couple who are subletting our apartment in Brooklyn. I gave them Peter's address so that they could forward any mail to him. When the letter came from a law firm, Peter thought he had better deliver it in person."

"No other way to reach you old chap, considering there is no phone at this place. We called the law firm before we headed north. We did not want to trouble you for some trifle."

"What they told us did not sound like a petite trifle," explains Michelle.

"Thank you both, I needed to get this letter, but I don't know how to help them. I have to, somehow. Mary has lived in that apartment since she was a baby, and it's the only home I've ever had."

Mick still looks puzzled so I explain, "Remember when we were in London, and we were wondering why someone would kidnap the Queens dogs, and focus negative attention to France? It did not make sense until we figured out that the Olympics were scheduled to be held in France and then, because of all the negative publicity, the US got the contract to host the summer Olympics. Well the guy who helped the US get the contact was a Mr. Miller. He's the same guy who owns all of the property in my neighborhood. They're the only low to middle income apartments left in the Prospect Heights neighborhood. This guy has wanted to tear it all down and build expensive condos. Now he has the chance. New York politicians gave him the contract to build in Brooklyn. He is displacing hundreds, if not thousands of people. I have to do something." I can't stop crying. Peter holds me and I get his shirt wet from my tears. I hate feeling helpless when someone needs me.

Michelle puts several papers on the table in front of Molly. "This is some of the information we have been able to find that might help people understand what is happening."

Molly reads the headlines, "Displacements world-wide caused by Olympics."

"Pierre told me what the lawyer said, and I did some research for you on the web. Under, 'Who benefits from the Olympics' I found..." Michelle picks up the papers and begins to read, "According to this report, '20 million people have been displaced over the last 20 years in preparation for the Olympic Games: Seoul Korea, 1988, 720,000 people were forcibly evicted from their homes. Barcelona Spain, 1992, housing became so unaffordable as a result of the Olympic Games that low income earners were forced to leave the city. Atlanta, Georgia, 1996, some 30,000 persons were displaced by Olympics related gentrification and development. Athens, Greece, in 2004, hundreds of Roma residents were displaced for Olympics related preparations.

In the lead is the 2008 Olympic Games in Beijing, China, over 1.25 million people were displaced due to Olympics-related urban redevelopment.' "

"This is unbelievable. I have to do something, but what can I do, I'm three thousand miles away."

"Think of your training Bridget. First you must calm you mind so that you can think clearly."

Mick patiently waits while I take several deep breathes. Then he asks, *"Bridget, what caused the world to change its mind against France as the major contender for the next Olympics?"*

"The negative news about the dog-napping in England, and how it *might* be related to the French."

"Exactly! Now get in touch with Mary and your other friends. Tell the world what is happening."

"You mean social network, like 'YouTube', 'Facebook', email, twitter..."

"Exactly, all the media was used to spread the news from London. Tell them all to spread the word of what is happening in Brooklyn."

"He is correct Bridget. Someone is sure to see the value in picking up the cause and running with it," Peter agrees.

I hug Mick and rush to my laptop.

"Wait, we don't have an internet connection on the island. I'll need to take the ferry to the village of Fionnphort and hope they have internet service."

"Bridget, come to Edinburgh with us. We will love to spend some time with you and show you the town. We have a special reason to go there." Peter looks over and winks at Michelle.

"I don't know how safe that will be..." says Mick so that all except Michelle can hear him.

"Pierre and I will go with you Bridgette. It will give us some time together. We can pick a great hotel and have dinner. A place to celebrate our good news," Michelle says as she waves her ring finger in the air. Peter hugs Michelle and announces, "We are going to be married. We have a couple of places in Edinburgh to take a look at for possible locations for the ceremony."

"You might say Scotland is neutral ground for both of our families." Michelle laughs.

Molly and I rush over to hug them and have Michelle show us her ring. I have never seen Peter so happy. His dark brown eyes are not as striking as Mick's golden honey orbs, but the happy glow is his and Michelle's faces are startling to witness. So this is what love looks like.

I look over at Mick and silently ask his okay to leave the Island. *"I would love to spend some time with them."*

"You will need your full concentration for the days ahead. Go lass, a day or two away will do you good but, please be careful. When you return, we will go to Ireland to assist your family."

Molly picks up on our silent conversation and announces. "Come along and pack an overnight bag. You will finally be able to wear some of your finery and get out of those jeans you have had to wear for training."

"Oui, I will help with the packing. Too bad we will not have time to go shopping in Edinburgh as we did in London," says my petite French fashionista. I thought *I* was clothes crazy. Her trip to a small island didn't stop Michelle from dressing to the hilt. You would think a veterinary assistant would wear jeans. I have never seen her in other than a dress or smart pant suit. Today is no exception.

She's wearing grey wool slacks with a two piece sweater set. So soft and flowing it must be cashmere. Around her neck is a fine, silk Hermes scarf with the perfect shades of lavender to set off her new doo. In London, she had her short, burgundy tinted hair streaked with black. Today she is a brunette with various shades of violet streaks woven in to give her hair style a top fashion look.

As we leave the room, I hear Mick ask Peter, *"How did Michelle take the news about the Fae Kingdom and your own special gift?"*

"After all that happened in London, I explained my gifts. I also explained Bridget's work with our ancestors. She took it very well. I think that most French people understand the Fae folk."

It took awhile to decide what to pack for an overnight stay in the glorious medieval city of Edinburgh, but after many grumbles from Mick and Peter, we were all set to head out.

INTERLUDE

Morrigan's Chamber
County Mayo, Ireland

The old fort has been taken over completely by Morrigan's creatures.

The only trace of color in the dark, cold chamber is the pale, eerie glow emanating from Morrigan's Celtic skin. Dressed all in black with dull, lifeless, black hair that falls below her waist, she sits on a stone throne and opens a portal to view Bridget from hundreds of miles away.

"Dagda appear!"

Dagda, angry at being woken at odd hours and grumpy by nature, materializes wearing a rumpled corporate business suit with sickle in hand. "Yes my Goddess, how may I be of assistance?"

"Bridget is away from the island, take her now."

"Yes my Goddess."

"Dagda?"

"Yes Goddess."

"No witnesses."

"Not a problem my Goddess, we will find the perfect setting for her capture."

CHAPTER 7

Bridget
Edinburgh, Scotland

"How do you like your room Bridgette?"

Michelle and I are sitting in my room, which has a separate lounge area. I look around at the beautifully decorated room done up in soft white and warm grey tones. The comfortable chairs and small round table are perfect for sending out my emails. I can't stop looking out the large window that offers breathtaking views over the Royal Mile.

"Thank you guys, I love it. It's perfect, the height of luxury and comfort. The Radisson Blu is an excellent choice. Please thank Peter for me. I didn't want you guys to pay for my room."

"No, no my sweet, this is our pleasure. If not for you, I would not have met my Pierre and since his recognition from the Queen he cannot keep up with all the work. He likes working for people who pay him so much. It leaves him time to work for people who cannot pay."

"I'm so glad all is working out for you guys. Are you still veterinary assist at Sandringham Palace for the Queen's Dorgis?"

"*Oui*, I love the Dorgis. Pierre would like me to be his assistant after we marry. I am thinking it over, we will see. I do love my Dorgis."

"How are the little scamps?"

"Ce Magnifique! Did you hear that the Queen of England has decided to stop breeding dogs because she's getting to that age where they might outlive her? She is an admirable person, so responsible. The Dorgis are a vital part of her life. I even heard that they sleep on her bed and when she is served her tea with scones that they get them. I spend a considerable deal of time exercising them to work off the calories," she laughs.

I laugh along with her and marvel at the change that has come over her. I remember Michelle sitting on the soaking wet steps of the 'Wedding Cake' outside Buckingham Palace, crying because she had been accused of dog-napping. Mick is right. When someone allows other people's opinions to get to them, they lose their life force, their inner glow. She has it back now. Before, I was a little jealous that she's so beautiful, now I'm so happy for her that there is no room for jealousy. I turn and admire the view from my window.

"This is the perfect spot, right on the Royal Mile. Later, when I'm done with all my emails, I'm going to walk the Royal Mile and visit St. Giles' Cathedral."

"You will wait for me to return to do the shopping at Jenners Department store on Princes Street. I have read about it. We will go," Michelle asks in her funny French way.

"It sounds as if Peter will keep you guys busy until late tonight. What was that he was saying about being King of his own Castle?"

"Oui, Fenton Tower is a 5 Star exclusive use venue. We will check it out for our wedding reception. Another place we are looking at is where the family will stay. It

is also a 5 Star venue, Lennoxlove House. It is a luxurious, stately home that has 11 bedrooms with centuries old architectural features."

"Wow how fancy. That should be some wedding."

"We love this city and think both of our families and friends will love it too. Why not make this a happy time for everyone? Perhaps you could talk the ghosties into letting us use the chateau?"

"Ghosties?" I laugh. I love talking with my French friend. "My family and friends, *the ghosties* don't want people knowing about them. Sorry, it won't be possible. If you talk about them, people will lock you up as crazy."

"*Oui,* my Pierre has warned me. You are correct no one would believe me."

Peter stands at the connecting door looking lovingly at Michelle.

"Are you ready then luv?"

Michelle goes to get her hat and coat. He comes over to hug me and warns, "You behave yourself now. Are you sure you don't want to come along? I hate to leave you on your own, but I need to get back to work to pay for all this, and we only have today."

"I will be okay, I promise."

"We will hurry."

"Don't you dare hurry, go enjoy yourselves! There are no subways here for Morrigan's creatures to push me onto the tracks, and I doubt if someone will shoot me with an arrow on the Royal Mile. Anyhow, my emails and phone calls with take forever, I'll be lucky to go to a café for lunch."

"Can you order in, that would be safer."

I laugh and push him out the door. Michelle returns wearing another remarkable creation. This one is a classic double-breasted trench coat in water resistant nylon paired with a jaguar printed lining for a bit of *Rive Gauche* flair, as she would say. It comes to just below her knees. I stare at the logo engraved horn buttons.

Michelle sees that I'm drooling over her coat. She says with a smile,

"*Oui*, it is a Yves Saint Laurent."

She laughs when I dramatically wave my arms in the air and bow down to her exquisite sense of style. After several more promises to be safe, I finally push them out the door.

I move my laptop to the table by the window, sit down and switch it on. While it's warming up I call Mary to break the awful news.

"Hey Mary, how are you doing?"

"I'm Grand!" she giggles when she uses the Irish expression.

I really hate to tell her about our apartment but I tell her about Peter and Michelle bringing the letter from the lawyer, about all of our neighbors being evicted and Mick's suggestions about social networking to stop the destruction of our old neighborhood.

"Bridge are you getting in touch with all the guys on the community watch committee?"

"Yeah I'm sending the emails now, but I wanted to talk it over with you. I still have most of the money I got from the lawyer in Ireland. If you want to fly over to Brooklyn and take on this fight in person, I can pay for the tickets. I know how upset it must be to lose the only home you've known. Heck, the only home I've known, but I can't go now. We are training for war. Can you believe it? A Fae War, unreal isn't it."

"I'm upset Bridge, but I can't just drop everything and fly to Brooklyn. I have work and other... responsibilities."

"Oh you mean Simon, how's he doing?"

"He left for Wales this morning and won't be back for a week. I'd love to come to see you someday... *if I can* get a break from work."

"Sure I'd love to see you anytime, you know that. When you come to Iona, you may need to rent a bike or you can try to rent a car. Drive a little past the Abbey. You will see a sign for Dun Hill. Park by Dun Hill, the gatekeeper makes a cottage appear for regular visitors but wait until you see what is actually there. It's a real live castle. Can you believe it! I can't wait to show you.

"Of course, you won't see the castle at first, but we will see you and open the portal. You'll love it. I was going to invite you and Simon after the war anyway.

"Wait, dang it, you'd better hold off until this war is over with. When you tell Simon about the Fae, he'll freak out and want to help us. I don't want to get him involved in this."

"I have been sort of hinting to Simon that your family is a little unusual." Mary laughs.

"Yeah, but it is best to wait awhile, not that we wouldn't love to see you guys. Heck Molly will go bonkers, but it might be safer. *And,* I want to be there to see Simon's face when he hears about the Fae," I laugh.

"Now boarding…"

"What is that, a loudspeaker? Mary, where are you?"

"Nothing, just going to surprise someone, got to go. Love ya girlfriend."

"Love ya but surprise who? Simon? You're going to Wales? Mary…"

Dang that girl, she hung up. I hope Simon appreciates what a fantastic lady he has.

I make myself a fresh cup of tea. With the mug steaming in my hand I check my G-mail.

Good grief, one hundred and thirty seven. Who has time to read all these. My ego does a nose dive when I read the *'From'* column. A hundred and thirty are junk mail. Some from my favorite shops, I ignore them for now. Oh well, seven is more manageable anyway.

Five are from neighbors wanting to tell me about the eviction notice they received. One is from the temp service wanting to know if I'm available for work.

Ah, this is more like it, an email from Helen. I sit back and relax. As the email opens I picture Helen as I last saw her in Ireland. Wife of my so called tenant, Connor Claffey, she'd been badly abused. Connor was not only trying to take the land I inherited but he was also a dangerous terrorist. I was so happy for Helen when he was arrested in London airport by Charlie Boyle. I take a sip of my tea and enjoy my email from Italy.

Dear Bridget,

I want to thank you again for giving me my life back. The money you loaned me...You gave me to pay forward, has come in handy. I stayed with my friend for the first week until I could find a position. I am now a 'Barista', can you believe it! I have to make that god-awful thick black stuff a million times a day. They thrive on it over here. My tip jar is always full, and the Italians love to flirt so much I feel more like a woman than a battering bag with every day that goes by.

The best news is that I joined a battered women's group. I have made many new friends. My best friend, Peggy, loves having me as her flat-mate. She refuses any rent money, so I am saving to start my own business. I am not sure what it will be yet. I want to be like you, and help others in need. If not for you ... well you know what happens to women that feel too helpless to leave.

I can run on and on about how happy I am. Thank you again for caring enough to reach out to me. I hope you come to Italy someday soon. I would love to give you the grand tour.

Ciao,
Helen

I feel so happy after the email update from Helen that I want to go out and enjoy this city. I hurry to reply to my neighbors. I group them into one email, and send them the statistics on dislocated people due to

Olympics, that Michelle found on-line. I also give them a few suggestions about the *possible*, underhanded way I thought the landlord might have gotten the deal for the Olympics. I warned them that he's probably not working alone, for them not to say anything to the city's politicians. I give them Charlie Boyle's contact information in England and ask my neighbors to get in touch with him, to see if he's able to track the money trail back to Mr. Miller.

When Charlie helped us capture a wanted terrorist in Ireland, he was promoted to detective inspector. When he and my cousin Peter received a Knighthood for the work they did in England, helping us save the Queen and St. Paul's Cathedral. I had to email my neighbors to tell them all about him.

They will probably squabble over who gets to contact him. Charlie is a big hero in their books. Too bad I couldn't tell them all what Mary and I did to help, but I told them enough to have them listen to my suggestions on how to save their homes.

If Charlie traces the money the dog-nappers were paid, back to Mr. Miller, and he is indicted, maybe that will slow up the process enough so that the city will have to look elsewhere to build. I "copy" Charlie on the email, so he will be up to date on what's happening.

I look at the screen and try to think of anything else I can do to help.

I send an email to Mrs. Slotnick. I ask her to have the movers move our belonging to the storage company she is using. I know that they will come to pack up and move her things anyway. I let her know that I'm paying for her management skills. She will receive a money order that will pay for both of our moving and storage fees, and I send money from my account to Western Union for Mrs. Slotnick.

I laugh out loud when I think of the look that will probably be on her face when she sees the amount. Born in the concentration camps, she still has the number they tattooed on her arm, but not on her heart. She is a fighter, and at her age she still wants to feel as if she is pulling her own weight and not taking handouts. She only retired a few years ago from The Caedmon Record Corporation. It's an uptown record company where she managed everything for forty years. I know that she'll be delighted to be paid for her management skills again.

I look at the list I made, that I entitled, *the Battle of Brooklyn*. Hmm must be all the talk of the Fae war. Well that's everything. I look outside and think that Michelle had the right idea, go out and enjoy this wonderful city.

It looks like rain so, I hurry and get dressed. Molly was so right it does feel wonderful to wear real clothes again, not just sweats or jeans for training. But somehow my usual clothes feel somewhat confining, and I feel self-conscious in them. I look in the mirror and admire my Ellen Tracy, belted, notched collar coat not as impressive as Michelle's YSL, but fabulous enough for me.

Funny each time I look in the mirror, I look different somehow, more healthy. Must be all that strenuous training Mick is putting me through, and the healthy food Molly cooks. Not only do I now have muscles but I look more like my mom. She is staring back at me. I don't remember when I developed this strong resemblance. Perhaps what I'm feeling inside is showing more on the outside.

When I first inherited the land in Ireland all I could think of was finding someone to take it off my hands. Fear was eating away at me. Fear of surviving in Brooklyn on my own. Fear of never having enough money. Heck I was giving away a home I'd inherited because of fear. Fear that I could not pay the taxes on the property, but most of all, fear that I was not good enough, or worthy enough to inherit anything.

The Fae believe in me. I'm training to help them but they have given me much more than I can ever pay back. They have taught me that fear kills.

Fear was killing me, little by little. I look like my mom now because I have the strength and courage of my ancestors. I straighten my back and shake my shoulder length hair and smile. "Dang this camel color goes perfect with my dark coloring and rosy cheeks, now to go show it off.

I walk down the 'Royal Mile', and stop at 'The Playhouse' to admire the architecture. A large poster reads, "Delve into the deep history of Scotland's capital and uncover secret tales and mystery at fantastic attractions such as *The Real Mary King's Close* before wandering the ancient streets of the Old Town or climbing Edinburgh's very own volcano - *Arthur's Seat.*"

Wow, I could spend a month here and not see everything. I walk to a café with outside tables and a fantastic view of Edinburgh Castle. I order one of Helen's 'thick black stuff' and just watch the people walking by.

I'm enjoying my coffee and turkey croissant sandwich, feeling terribly European. A girl that looks like a gypsy, all dark black hair, and the deepest blackest eyes I have ever seen, smiles and hands me a pamphlet. I thank her and read the large red headlines, 'See The Real Mary King's Close! Buried deep beneath Edinburgh's Royal Mile lays the city's deepest secret warren of hidden streets that have remained frozen in time since the 17th century. For hundreds of years, the true story of the Close has remained untold until now! In the company of an expert guide, you can explore this unique site, and experience what it was truly like for people who lived, worked and died here.'

At the bottom of the page, is a coupon for half price for the noon showing. I look at the time on my cell. I have fifteen minutes left to buy a ticket. Heck, it'll only take an hour, and I don't expect Peter and Michelle back until dinner time. And it's on sale. I smile as I hurry to the kiosk I noticed earlier in front of 'The Playhouse.'

This is a kick. I'm so glad I came. The two guides dressed in costumes from the 17th century are hysterical and have considerable information on all the places we pass. These narrow, ancient streets could certainly tell a story, and it would all be creepy. We pass an antique shop window. I stop to admire a Bellaresque, leather and gold chain bag. Wow 190€, wonder what that would be in dollars. I open my cell and check the calculator. Shocked by the price, I hurry to join my tour group, only I can't find them.

The buildings on these dark, narrow streets have hundreds of alleys between them. It is like a giant maze. I rush to the end of the street, and dig out my cell to use it as a GPS, and hopefully find my way back to the hotel. I guess I miss out on the rest of the tour I grumble to myself.

Dang, what bad luck, no signal, now what? I start walking along the empty streets holding my cell in front of me, hoping to pick up a signal.

A long, thin arm knocks my cell out of my hand and pulls me into the nearest alley. I attempt to scream, and no sound comes out.

Why is it that I can talk a blue streak when I'm mad? When I'm scared, I can't say a word.

It drags me to an open door. I know I don't want to go there. I remember what Mick said about concentrating on what you want, and it will happen. I break my arm free, turn to look at the creature that grabbed me. He is about seven feet tall and looks like the 'Icabod Crane' character, complete with 17th century attire. Creatures like this are from tales in dusty books, not real. He has the glazed look of one be-spelled. Like the man in Mayo and the one at the Tube station in London, this one is be-spelled to do Morrigan's biding. Hopefully it will wear off soon. My picture must be on some crazy 'Wanted Dead or Alive' wanted poster for all be-spelled creatures to see.

"What am I to do with you?" I fly away from him but before I gain any altitude I am swished out of the air by a tree limb.

"What the heck? She has be-spelled the trees also?" I cry as I fall to the ground and Icabod is joined by two casually dressed street thugs. They drag me into a fenced, private garden area. Icabod pushes me against a small pine tree. The two thugs wrap me in rope.

"Hah, these idiots were not told that I can do magic." Even without wiggling my nose, I vision the rope untangling from me and wrapping them up. I then picture the rope knotting around their waists and pulling them together. Then the rope lifts them in the air as it ties around a tree limb. Over the shouts of the two men I hear a funny sounding chuckle. I look around, it's not coming from Icabod. I walk towards him...

Behind me, I hear John Wayne say, "Care for some help little lady."

I turn and see a spirit in a monks robe standing next to one of my favorite ghosts.

"Friar Xavier, I'm so happy to see you."

I almost run and hug him but remember the bone chilling effect of a handshake and hold back. "Who is your friend? Please tell me that he isn't really John Wayne. That would be just too creepy."

"My dear, let me introduce you to Skeletor. I believe I mentioned him. He is the famous CCTV spirit caught on film."

Skeletor shutters and frowns at the mention of his unplanned TV appearance.

"I'm very happy to meet you Skeletor. Please excuse me for a second."

I turn to deal with the creature, and he's gone. Oh well.

"What brings you to Scotland Friar?"

"I thought it best if Skeletor took a holiday. You heard him. He is now addicted to the telly."

"Yeah."

I laugh at Skeletor's perfect imitation of the Fonz.

"I gather someone at the palace is into old time television shows."

"Wait till you hear him speak like Lucille Ball," the Friar laughs.

"Where are you guys staying, want to come back to the hotel with me? Michelle would love to know you are in the same room as she is."

"We would love to dear, but we are staying at the Palace at Holyroodhouse. You see it is the anniversary of the day that Mary, Queen of Scots witnessed her jealous second husband, Lord Darnley, brutally kill her secretary Rizzio. Skeletor listens to Rizzio while I attempt to console dear Queen Mary."

"How horrible, I'll explain to Michelle, she will understand. She and Peter will expect you at their wedding. Will you be able to attend?"

"Of course my dear, unless our Prince Charles gets himself into a pickle, I will be there."

"Ah Friar, would you happen to know the way back to my hotel?"

"We will be honored to escort you my dear, won't we Skeletor?"

As we walk along, I tell the good Friar and Skeletor all about my training for the upcoming Fae war.

"What I can't understand is why the Fae are killing each other."

"My dear, the Fae are not harming each other, it is a rule that immortal, magical beings cannot do harm to another."

"I know that I send them to the holding place until the spell rubs off, but I *have* turned a couple of her creatures to dust."

"From dust we are made, and to dust we will return. The creatures are returned to their original size and place on this earth. Please understand, you do no harm, but are doing what is needed to return order to our world. I am afraid Morrigan has caused much disruption."

"How do we stop Morrigan? Steal her magic spell book or something?"

"Wish it was that easy my dear. Morrigan is a vile deity of chaos restricted by no moral code whatsoever. From what you have told me, it sounds as if she takes harmless creatures like newts, bats, and whatever she comes across and be-spells them to grow in size and convinces them to fight for her side."

"How does she convince them?"

"Mere words. The greatest leaders were masters of the spoken word, both for good and for evil. Remember your history. Hitler was a simple wallpaper hanger. He spoke to groups of people using only the strength of his words. With only his words, he built an army that caused mass destruction. Words have always had power. Unfortunately, many do not realize when they are under someone's power. Often people look for their basic needs to be met. They want friends or companionship. So they choose to accept the words. Morrigan is using the Fae to use words to bring about world war. She is using words to be-spell, or some would say she hypnotizes humans to do her biding."

"How can you make sure it doesn't happen to you? You know...be taken over by another Hitler."

"Faith and adhering to simple words written two thousand years ago, 'Do unto others as you would have them do unto you.' Any belief that behooves you to hurt, shame, even ignore another human being is not what was meant by those words. Put simply they mean to do no one harm in any way."

Skeletor looks at our sad faces and says in Ethel's voice, "Morrigan and Hitler are cut out of the same mold." Then he switches to Lucy's voice and says, "Yeah, and they're getting moldier."

I'm still laughing when we arrive at the hotel. Because of the crowd of people walking the Royal Mile in search of an early dinner, I make sure to mind-speak my goodbyes.

We are up early the next morning to shop and see a few sights before we take the ferry to Iona.

"Thank you guys for coming with me, it was fun to take a day off and sightsee in Edinburgh. This place certainly has some great history."

"They have so many ghosts here that 'The Edinburgh Ghost Fest' was launched by Mary King's Close, a Scottish Tourist Board." Michelle laughs.

"We must see that."

"When you were busy with your emails this morning, Michelle dragged me to Edinburgh Castle. It is situated on the West outcrop of the ancient volcano that makes up Arthur's Seat. It is one of the most famous of all Edinburgh landmarks. Thousands of tourists visit it every year. As well as the historic Edinburgh Castle, it is also one of the most haunted places in Scotland," Peter laughs.

"Laugh all you want. I know there are ghosties. Didn't you tell me about the Friar in London who asked Bridgette to come to my aid?"

"My dear, I didn't say that there are no ghosts, but I doubt they appear in these large numbers."

I grab Peter's arm, "Don't laugh cuz, that's an ancient castle, there may be as many ghosts as they claim. I have my hands full right now, but someday I'll visit the castle, and find out how many there actually are," I laugh.

"Did I tell you guys that one of the emails I got this morning was from Mrs. Larson, my upstairs neighbor? She said that they got the students at Brooklyn College involved and they have scheduled protests.

"One neighbor is meeting with the City officials to offer alternative sites. Hopefully if they choose one of these alternative sites than fewer people, if any will be displaced."

"That is great news Bridgette."

"What alternative sites are they suggesting?"

"According to Mrs. Larson, one recommendation is the 646 acre site of the 1939-40 New York's World's Fair and later the unofficial, 1964 New York World's Fair at Flushing Meadow in Queens, New York. Another possible site is my favorite, the Gold Coast. I think it is in Suffolk County, NY on Long Island."

"Why is that your favorite?" Peter asks.

"The Gold Coast is appropriately named. It is home to numerous historic mansions that are open to the public. Homes built by the Vanderbilts and others in their pay range. Those estates are so large they already have Olympic size swimming pools, tennis courts, and no one will be displaced. Heck, I would pay good money to go to see the Olympics' in those settings."

"Sounds like the data you sent them from my research was the fuel needed to slow down the process, so officials have time to think before they destroy people's homes."

"Of course what they build will be much prettier than the gang graffiti you mentioned."

"Correct but you can't sleep in a million dollar stadium. There have to be homes for people."

I look over and see the afternoon ferry to Iona pulling into port.

"You don't need to come back with me. I'll be safe from here. Go back to work. Remember you have to pay for that fantastic wedding. I don't want to be Maid of Honor at just any old place."

The ferry to Iona is small, since only foot traffic is allowed. I allow my mind to wander and look around me. The steel grey boat has large, floor to ceiling windows that give passengers a magnificent view and protects them from the crisp ocean breeze. The sign gave the maximum capacity at eighty, but I think the cold steel chairs and benches would only hold half that number. Right now it looks almost full, and I only count twelve people.

I watch the waves from the safety of the cabin for a short while then I'm drawn outside. Avoiding the people at the front of the boat, I find a secluded section in the back. The wind whips at my hair and clothes until they're wrapped around me, but the feel of the waves, and scent of the sea give me a sense of peace, and a totally unexpected sense of freedom. I guess I've been under a lot of stress worrying about the upcoming war. It isn't until I feel my muscles begin to relax that I realize how stressed I've been and how seldom I've been alone lately. I watch the waves and let my thoughts ramble.

I'm happy for Peter and Michelle and enjoy being with them, but somehow I knew I had to take the ferry back by myself, I need some alone time. In the past I would often escape the crowds of the city, and take a ride on the Staten Island ferry. Just ride back and forth, always standing at the rail no matter what the weather. The sea has the most relaxing effect on me.

It was nice having their company on the ferries, buses and trains we had to take just to get to Edinburgh, especially when that woman in the red jacket pushed against me at the train station. I was reminded of the enthralled man who attempted to push me onto the tracks in front of an oncoming train in London. Luckily Peter grabbed my arm or I would have had a nasty fall and ruined another outfit.

The sea is mesmerizing. I feel at one with nature, a small part in the greater plan. I know that no matter what the greater plan is, I will do my best to play an active part in it. I need to remember that I'm worthy, and I have a purpose. I'm part of the plan, no matter what it is.

I'm distracted from my inner soul searching by a flash of red. I feel a hand on my back and a hard push, next thing I know I'm getting wet from the ocean's spray. It all happens in a split second before I can think of magic. All of a sudden I'm grabbed by two strong arms and we are flying back onto the boat. My front is wet from the ocean spray and from being held against a rock hard body. I look at the hunk in front of me and see Johnny Depp. The only difference is he's shaped like a body builder and sounds like Sean Connery. I push back away from him and sit on a steel bench. He sits down beside me.

"Are you okay miss?"

"I think so."

I look over at two other Johnny Depp look-a-likes holding the woman in the red jacket.

"Please don't hurt her, she is enthralled by Morrigan. She will snap out of it."

"Not to worry miss, my mates are handling matters."

"Thank you for your help. I could fly out of the ocean, but that may have been after I ruined my outfit. I don't think anyone recommends washing suede in saltwater."

I grin at Mr. Muscles hoping to get a smile in return.

"Aye. My name is Andrew, and you are Bridget I take it."

"I am, how do you know...oh, Mick. I did tell him that I was making the crossing by myself."

"He said you would land yourself in trouble. You are too valuable for the Selich of Orkney not to watch out for."

I start to ask questions, but he sees that we are nearing land and says, "They are expecting a Fae war on Orkney and Shetland Islands. We have offered our assistance. You may be needing to assist those folks at Stonehenge and hereabouts."

"Me...I can't...A Selich?"

"Aye, you may know us as Selkie."

"Seal people. I have heard many stories but never knew they were true."

"Now some of it is, and some of it isn't."

He smiles at me and I'm ready to swoon. He looks around, nods his head to his companions, leans over and kisses me on the cheek.

"Be good now lass. We are all counting on ya."

Next thing I know we're pulling into dock. The lady with the red jacket is in line ready to depart and my selkies are nowhere to be seen. I'm happy that the one story I read of them appearing naked was wrong. He sure looks sensational in the diving suit.

I wait until the end to depart, putting as much distance between me and red jacket as possible. I shouldn't have worried. Niamh and Tristan are standing by what looks like a fancy golf cart. I walk up to Niamh and Tristan.

"Wow, what a ride, thank you guys for meeting me."

Chapter 8
Back to Training
I meet a Bunny with Attitude

"Today you need to learn to hide in plain sight and find your way around the forest."

"You do realize that at just under 5 foot 6 inches tall, I'm by no means tall but I'm not the size of a dog?"

We're walking in the woods beyond the castle. I turn around to argue some more with Mick and he's gone. "Okay, come out, come out wherever you are."

No response. I walk around some more then sit on a patch of grass in the sunlight. "Okay Mick, where are you?"

"Right here." Mick says inches away from my face.

"How did you do that?"

"Bridget we are in the woods. There are many places to hide but you do have the magical ability to cloak yourself. Make yourself invisible for short periods of time."

"You're kidding right? I can do that? Like that chick on 'Fantastic Four'. Will I materialize naked?"

"Ah, no."

"Okay, what are the magic words?"

"You really must stop reading fantasy novels."

"Sure, okay, what now?"

"Concentrate on what you want to happen and it will."

After several tries, I get the hang of it and actually see my hand disappear... talk about freaky.

"We will need to work more on that. Now I am going to leave you here and you need to return to the castle on your own."

"No way Jose, that ain't happening. I'm from Brooklyn, remember. I don't do woods. The last couple of times I was in the woods I ruined two great pair of shoes."

No response.

"Mick, don't leave me here. How do I find my way back?"

I walk through the woods for several minutes calling for Mick. I know he won't leave me. He is too worried about Morrigan's creatures.

"Mick, get back here, we're wasting valuable time."

"You tell him girl."

"What?"

"Ain't that just like a man, gone as soon as you need them. Don't worry honey child, you're as safe in these here woods as if you were in your mammy's arms."

"What?"

"Aha, it must be a man you're yellin' at, your brain has quit... You never can trust a man, you know that girl. They is always lyin.

"How can you tell?"

"If their lips are a flappin' then they is lyin."

I keep looking but I can't find who I'm speaking with.

"If you are a spirit, could you materialize? It feels weird not seeing who I'm speaking with."

"And why isn't you seeing me, you got eyes ain't ya?"

"What the heck?"

"There you goes again, must be that man trouble."

"Momma, Keirney won't play with me."

"Go on honey child, we have a sad lady here, she is blind and has man troubles."

"She is big, Momma."

"Most humans are big, just talk to their feet Bradlee, they's all our size then."

"Momma, Brianne got dirt on me."

"Momma, Kaelea and Ashton won't play with me."

"Chillan, go play now, I've got me some serious woman talk here."

"Yes Momma. Can we go talk to Toadie?"

"Sure but Karin, you run along now and watch that the young'ins don't get too close to that old Toadies' pond."

"Yes Momma."

I sit down on the ground in shock. There are a dozen rabbits running around. The large one must be the Momma Bunny. I can hear them talking. Some are black and white, some have floppy ears, some have the largest ears I have ever seen and the one coming over is the strangest rabbit I have ever seen.

Que-tip said that I could talk with animals but I never tried. Maybe since I'm in their home territory it comes naturally. The larger rabbit comes over and stands right in front of me. She has a round face and short ears, long white and rust colored fur. Her whiskers are twitching a mile a minute.

"Can you see me now honey child?"

"Yes, Ms. Bunny, but why do you talk that way. Shouldn't you have a Scottish accent?"

"Now honey child, haven't you ever heard of special imports? I is special, I'm from Collinsville, Mississippi, the home of the Lion head rabbit."

"What brings you to Iona, Scotland?"

"Well that's a story to be told. There was this here record star. She has this big old bus and it breaks down in Brandon. While they is fixing it she wanders into a store where they have me and my young'ins in a cage. Those people were fixin on havin us for dinner don't you know. Well now this lady, Va-Nissa is her name, she rescued us and sent us to this here sanctuary for bunnies."

"What got you so upset with the male species?"

"What's not to be upset with, they is male right, always up to somethin."

She looks over to check on her youngsters playing with the largest, fattest toad I've ever seen. The toad is croaking out what I think is a song, jumping in the pond and splashing the bunnies. They are running and laughing.

"Ms. Bunny, do you know the way back to the castle?"

"I sure is sorry but Miss Judith will know the way."

"Who is Miss Judith?"

The bunny hops around in glee and is laughing up a storm singing, "Who, Who. That is Miss Judith, Who, Who."

Just then, a beautiful white, large owl, with dark grey marking comes over and lands on the branch above my head.

"Did you call?"

"Hi Miss Judith, this poor little lamb is lost, can you or your young'ins see her on her way back to the castle?"

"Who, my young...Ah... Ashlee and Emily are busy at their lessons, I will do the honors."

Miss Judith flies low to the ground and looks up at me. "Hmm, I had better perch on your arm."

I hold my arm out for Miss Judith and say good-bye to my new friends.

"Wow, I can't believe I'm talking with the animals. I got Doctor Doolittle beat, that's for sure."

"Doctor Doolittle?"

"Sorry, Miss Judith, I was just thinking out loud. How do you like living in the woods?"

"The enchanted woods around the castle are a very safe place for all of us."

"Ms Bunny thinks it is a bunny sanctuary."

"Oh it is a sanctuary for all of us. Unfortunately there are very few places left on earth as sanctuaries. I can understand when there is actual hunger, that one would hunt and kill living things to feed their family. Unfortunately many hunt and kill us just for sport. Some kill us in large numbers and leave us where we lay, not even proud to show us. Just want to kill us because they can. The faeire who brought both Ms Bunny and me here is Lynne, the faeire I believe you met in England."

"Yes, I know Lynne. She is Que-tip's buddy and one of the 'communication squad'" I laugh. "Her home base is Stonehenge, how did you know we met?"

"Whenever Lynne visits the castle she comes out into the woods and talks with us. We know all about Mick and the upcoming Fae war. We also know how important your role is. We love watching you train, we haven't had such a good laugh in ages."

"Hmm, thanks, glad I could help," I laugh.

Mick comes into the dining room while I'm telling Niamh all about Ms. Bunny and her attitude about men.

"I see you had no problem finding your way back."

"You're right, it was fun. I love talking with the animals."

"Bridget met Ms Bunny and Miss Judith," Niamh laughs. "Ms. Bunny does not like men who lie, isn't that interesting."

Mick looks at Niamh. *"If you are both finished eating we still have some daylight left for training."*

INTERLUDE

Simon, Running Dog Inn
Glasgow, Scotland

"Thank you for meeting with me Alan."

"Now brother, don't worry we will find your lady. You mentioned that your Mary passed through Glasgow Monday on her way to Iona?"

"Yes, to visit her friend Bridget. She is the only family she has left. Mary's mother took Bridget in when Bridget's father died. They have spent the last twelve years together. They are as close as sisters. Bridget must know where Mary is."

"Have you tried speaking with Bridget?"

"There is no phone service on the island. I asked the local constable to stop by the cottage where she is staying. The young lady there said that Bridget was in Edinburgh. She is expected back today."

"Are you certain that Mary arrived in Iona?"

"Yes, the surveillance footage at the airport shows her passport being stamped arriving in Glasgow. She purchased a ticket for the ferry to Iona, but there is no record of return purchase."

"What do they say on the island?"

"I am on my way over to the Island now. When the constable checked the island a few days ago, he found no sign of Mary. I have been in touch with Bridget's cousin. He and his fiancée will meet me at the Ferry and come to the island with me. I will finally be able to speak with Bridget, and then perhaps I will have a lead."

"I have Mary's picture and will go door to door if I must. We will find her."

"I appreciate you leaving your family and making the trip over to assist me."

Simon pauses and walks to the window. "Mary is looking forward to meeting you and the family. We planned to come to invite you to the wedding in person."

Simon looks at his phone again.

"Mary wanted to be with me when we made the announcement. We are to be married this December, in London."

Alan reaches over and hits Simon on the arm.

"Good work brother mine, glad to hear that you are finally settling down. It will be grand. Does our mother know the news?"

"Not yet and don't breathe a word. She will be put out not being the first to know…. Mary had it all planned, first her friend in Iona…"

"Mum's the word old sod. Can't wait to meet her, I know we will find her. Then you both can come by the house and mention it all official like, after you tell our mother."

"She will like that."

Alan stands to leave and Simon clasps his hand. He sits back down and tries his mobile again.

"Would you like more coffee sir?"

"No, thank you."

As the waiter leaves Simon stares at the silent mobile phone in his hand, still no message from Mary.

He checks his incoming messages and dials. "Alan, Simon here, I am still at the Running Dog. The constable I sent to Iona received a report via postal service. The rental people on the island wish to file a report of a stolen bicycle. He recognized Mary's name and thought I would like to know."

"Then your instincts are correct. She is on the Island."

"Something has happened either on the island, or ...."

"Would you rather I come to the Island with you?"

"No, please continue checking the area. If she has been taken, then they may have come this way. If I run into difficulties, I will come get your assistance."

"Did the rental people mention where Mary was headed when she left their shop?"

"She said she was going to her friend's home near the Abbey. She planned to return the bike in a few days. I am worried that she may have had an accident. I have checked all hospitals in Scotland. Pulled some strings and have an APB out for her as a missing person of interest. I had Iona send out a patrol to check the area surrounding the Abbey, but no sign of Mary or an accident. As of today, she has been gone ten days."

"Right, I am on it! I am beginning my leg work now. Don't worry brother, we will find her."

"Does she have any family we should notify?" a dazed Peter asks.

"What? Family?   No, we were to marry. We were planning a family. She must be on the island. We will find her."

"Simon we will be at the island shortly. We were here last week. We know the way. Your constable only spoke with the gatekeeper. There is a great deal I need to tell you before we arrive. I promise you that Bridget has the resources to find her. Come on deck where we can speak privately. Who knows man, she may be with Bridget now. This lack of communication technology on the Island makes me feel sorry for the dark ages. How do those people manage without mobile coverage?"

"Simon, I know Bridgette will find her."

Michelle holds Simon's arm to comfort him.

"What you will do is get some decent food in you and some rest. It will do no one any benefit if you drop over dead now, will it? I will go get you a snack while my Pierre explains the magic."

CHAPTER 9

Mary is missing
Iona, Scotland

Mick and Molly materialize in the parlor where Bridget was speaking with Simon, Peter, and Michelle.

"Bridget, what is it? What is wrong? Did you call for help."

I turn to Mick. I'm so relieved to see him. He may be a dog, but he's so smart, I know he can help. All I can do now is cry, I can't even think straight.

"Bridget, you look as if you are ready to pass out. Please come, have a seat and tell me what is wrong."

"I think Morrigan has my friend Mary. I just spoke with Simon. He's going nuts. He's been looking for her for days and can't find her. She was supposed to be *here* last Friday, then return to their flat in London, and meet Simon when he returned from Wales. That was last Monday, when I spoke with her. She was coming here. She wanted to surprise me. Mick, she's been missing ten days."

"Perhaps Simon missed something..."

"Simon's a British spy and his brother Alan is a Chief Inspector. They didn't miss anything. He has everyone helping him look. They can't find her."

"Where was the last place he saw her?"

"She was coming here. She arrived on Iona. They had no cars to rent, so she rented a bike. That is the last time they saw her. She was coming to see me." I cried. "She never got here, and her bike was never returned."

"Tristan, Niamh, you are needed."

Within a second, both stand before Mick.

"Gather your crew members, spread the word that Bridget's friend Mary is missing from Iona, I want her found within the hour. Then return here."

Both nod and leave as quickly as they materialized.

"I thought it was only the Fae or those with Fae blood, like me who weren't safe. She was after me!"

"I may have misjudged Morrigan's resourcefulness."

"We don't even look alike. Mary's blonde and I've brown hair. She's also taller and thinner."

I look into the golden eyes of the best friend I've ever had besides Mary. I know he will find her.

"Where is Simon?" Mick and Molly ask at the same time.

"When Bridgette told Simon that Mary wasn't here, he and my Pierre took the rental to search the island," Michelle explains.

"We will spread the word with others, we will find her," an anxious Molly says. "Come along with me Michelle, I have a wee bit of explaining to do."

"*Oui*, Mollie, are you a ghostie?"

"Now my dear in France you call us...." Molly explains as they leave.

"Mick, why take Mary, I don't understand?"

"Bridget, your friend was captured in Iona the same day you were scheduled to return from Edinburgh. She must have taken the earlier ferry. You arrived on the later ferry. You are both on Iona, in Scotland."

"This is a small island. Morrigan wouldn't have any trouble finding me here, why didn't she come after me instead of Mary?"

"Morrigan never does her own dirty deeds. She would have sent her creatures. They were told the basics, a Yank on the Island of Iona. This is a remote part of Scotland. Her creatures are not known for their intelligence. Somehow they found her instead of you."

"Mick things are just starting to go well for Mary. She nursed her mom day and night for two whole years. She had to watch her die and couldn't do anything to stop the cancer from growing. We couldn't do anything," I cried. "That's why she had to work from home, and why she doesn't have many friends. After her mom died, a part of us died too. Don't you see, she is just starting to live. She loves Simon, and he loves her. They are planning a life together. She has to be okay! She has to!"

"Your intuition tells you that she is alive. We will find her. We will get all the details. We will narrow our search. Once Morrigan discovers her mistake..."

He didn't finish saying what he was thinking, but I know. Once Morrigan discovers her mistake, what reason would there be to keep Mary alive? We have to find her before that happens.

Mick is speaking with Tristan. *"Is there any word?"*
"Nothing yet, have you more details for us?"

"Yes, she was seen biking off the A68, a dirt road near the Abbey. Come back here and we will drive the surrounding area."

Tristan is driving a car he must have manifested. It is definitely not the rental we returned. It has no annoying GPS. I guess Simon has that one. Simon won't give it up until he finds Mary. Hope no one else needs the car. Niamh is in the passenger seat. Mick and I are in the back seat. The car window is open to help me feel better. Being sick to my stomach is the pits. Mick is right; all this worry is making me sick. I try to admire the incredible scenery as we drive along the county road that Mary rode on her rented bike. We turn a corner and are now in darkness, as a canopy of trees shades the road.

"I don't like how this area feels, hmm, sort of creepy."

Mick looks at me and shouts, *"Stop the car."*

Tristan jams on the brake, and Niamh falls against him. She glowers at Tristan. He smiles and winks at her.

"What's up?" I ask.

"When you have a feeling about a place, it's good to investigate."

"Even a bad feeling?"

We exit the car and Mick starts to sniff the ground. I walk over to a young tree lying alongside the road. "I wonder why this one fell."

Tristan comes over to investigate. "It did not die naturally. Someone killed it."

He points to the base of the tree, showing me where it was hacked down. "A young tree does not have the skill of the ancients."

"If they wanted to cut this young tree then why didn't they take the wood to use?"

Mick comes over, sniffs the tree then runs up the hill, into the clearing and back to the road.

"Mary was here. From the road, I can follow her scent to the clearing. Then it vanishes."

"Any other scent, do you smell Morrigan?"

"I did find Mary's bike and bag. They are hidden under a pile of leaves."

"Where is she?"

Mick leans against me, *"There is something else. I smell blood, a lot of blood."*

"I know she's alive, we've got to keep looking."

We walk for about a mile. I notice a somewhat hidden driveway in a bend in the road. "Let's check this out."

Mick, Tristan and Niamh, exchange a look but follow me onto the drive. We walk a short way and see a hidden entrance leading to a building on the Abbey grounds.

"Not a place I expect to find Mary, it looks like an Inn. Maybe it is used as a retreat house, which is why it is hidden from view. I believe we need to check it out."

"Let's keep walking."

The Abbey's Inn is three stories of light and dark brown stone with corner turrets and bow windows. A grand entrance includes a stone arched portico with lanterns that are almost a full story tall on either side of the opening.

We all walk to the entrance, expecting any moment for someone to come out with a shotgun to get us off their property.

I stop, and Mick asks, *"What is it Bridget?"*

"I don't think it's lived in."

"It is a rental, rented out for groups of visitors or weddings and such."

We continue walking across the front lawn to the side away from the driveway. As I turn to walk towards the back, Mick stops and bends his head to the ground.

"Keep walking Bridget."

I walk in front of Mick. I can hear him sniffing the ground directly behind me. Tristan and Niamh are standing off to the side. Mick is so close I can feel his breath on my leg.

"What are you doing? Are you sniffing my butt?"

Mick is in shock. He stands still, mouth open. Tristan and Niamh almost collapse laughing.

"Hey, what's so funny guys? That's a dog thing, right?"

I realize that I'm standing with my hands on my hips and glaring at Mick. He shakes his head and explains.

"This area was recently taken by Morrigan. She has shielded the entire area. Where you step, the shield

*evaporates. I have picked up Mary's scent. Keep walk-
ing."*

Mick lowers his nose to the ground, following my
footsteps. I come to the end of the building.

"Got anything?"

*"She was here. Keep walking to the tower of the Mac
Gil."*

"Where?"

"Walk around the back to the far turret."

Mick stops. *"Wait here."*

He continues around with is nose to the ground. The
few minutes feel like hours. He comes over and stands
by me.

"How are you holding up my girl?"

"Mary has had a rough life, enough of fear, she
deserves better."

*"She wouldn't be who she is now without the life's
lessons she's been given."*

I frown at that comment, but think over what he
said, "I never thought about it that way before."

*"It is the only way to think about it...look for the
positive. There is always something, somewhere, even if
it's sometimes tough to find it. Sometimes it is hard to
see the good in a situation until years down the road."*

"Yeah?"

Mick nods.

"I've heard that philosophy before Mick. I have to tell
you, I'm not sure I buy into it. If everything has a
positive side, then what's positive about Mary missing?"

*"I do not know Mary's path. We cannot figure out
someone else's issues, only our own. We can try, but we*

would only be guessing. When things happen where you can't see any good side, it's usually best to focus on things where you can. Hold on to the good."

"That's tough to do right now."

"Bad stuff happens. The question is, do you focus on it and feel worse or try to find reasons to feel okay in spite of it?"

I nod thoughtfully. "Doesn't it seem callous to try to feel okay when someone you care about may be in trouble?"

"Does your wallowing in her situation make you feel any better?" Mick asks.

"No."

"Then what is the point of being miserable then?"

"That's the most unique prospective I've ever heard."

"It is my prospective on life. The way I see things, does not mean that anyone else needs to agree. But if it helps keep your energy and spirit up, then I suggest you try it on for size."

"What is this all about, this lesson to stay positive, why here, why now?"

"When one is running on heart energy for long periods of time there is a strain on all parts of the body. You need all of your energy to flow to the brain. Let the heart be at peace. Let the mind work at its best."

Tension, which had curled into a tight little knot in my belly, began to uncoil. Mick looked into my eyes, and then moved forward with his warm body pressed closer to me for comfort. I'm instantly overcome by a feeling of relief. My taut nerves seem to relax, my muscles unclench. I feel warmth right to my core. I lean against him and close my eyes, and just for one moment, the pain stops. I let the hurt and fear of the day, flow out of me. It's as if Mick is siphoning it off, taking it into himself instead.

INTERLUDE

Morrigan's Chamber
Mistaken Identify

The clouds move to show the vision in the portal. It reveals Bridget on the Abbey grounds with Mick.

Morrigan's anger erupts across the sky. Thunder roars. Lightning cracks. She screams, "Get a message to those simpletons. What is wrong with them? Do I have to do everything myself? I want Bridget. That is not her in the cage!"

Morrigan shouts at the vision in the portal, "You will not win. Soon all Fae will be mine."

She raises her staff in the air and shouts.

"Dagda appear!"

Dagda, appears as a corporate executive, except for the sickle of death he carries.

"Yes Goddess?"

Morrigan ignores Dagda as she spots a young elf sneaking across the land; she raises her staff and points it at the elf. The elf is turned to a green stone statue.

"It is time. We war against the Fae Kingdom."

Dagda holds back a sigh clearly tired of Morrigan's temper tantrums. He looks at the scenes being played out within the portal.

"Look upon the vision Goddess. The Queen's mortal form has faded. She will no longer be able to use humans to stop your plans."

Morrigan sits and glares at Dagda.

"We war now."

Dagda changes the vision to that of a bloody battle scene.

"Enjoy the view my Goddess. Your be-spelled Fae are causing wars among the mortals."

"I want a Fae war."

Morrigan stands and paces. Dagda holds back his anger at Morrigan's demands.

"My wise Goddess, you have said tis better to use your cousins Fae for our purposes. Her continued weakening and pain at their loss does bring you happiness."

Morrigan looks at Dagda, "It does."

Morrigan walks to Dagda and what he sees in her eyes make him tremble.

"We will rid the world of the Fae queen and her followers now!"

"Yes, my Goddess."

CHAPTER 10

Captured
The Abbey, Iona, Scotland

Once we are out of sight of the drive and main road, Mick looks at Tristan and Niamh.

"Your help is needed."

Tristan and Niamh begin to change. They drop the glamour of the modern age. Their clothes disappear. Their wings appear. I usually see wings when the Fae take on a smaller size, but to see wings now, this close and at this much larger scale, is like looking at an incredible, human size, work of art. It's fantastic. Niamh's skin is turning to a fluorescent white with aqua-silver swirls. Her wings match her skin tone but have shades of pink and lavender added. Tristan's skin is turning various shades of green. His wings have an added shade of gold.

I stop and stare. Mick nudges me forward with his nose. We all come to a stop around a curve about a half mile from the Abbey entrance. We're at a gate to a turret.

"Mary is being held captive in the dungeon under this portion. We cannot delay."

"What's happening to her?"

"The longer she is under Morrigan's influence, the harder it will be to break her free."

"Where is Morrigan, is she here?"

"*I cannot tell. Her magic is so strong it may just be residual magic that I smell, or she may be in residence.*"

"How do we get Mary?"

"*We will get her, you return to the car. We cannot afford to lose you. Tristan and Niamh will go in after her.*

"But..." I begin to protest and look at Niamh. She is wearing a white silk mini-dress over fluorescent skin. She reaches into her white Afro and draws what looks like a long, lethal hat-pin from her hair. She walks to where Mick stands. She makes a single stab to her arm. I continue to stare and feel a wet nose on my leg nudging me back to the car.

"I'm going with them. Mary is in trouble because of me."

Mick looks at me and nods. He walks to a point ten feet from Niamh and nods to Tristan, whose skin is a forest green. He wears a moss green shirt and pants, with a green Robin Hood style hat, across his back is a quiver of arrows and a bow. Tristan walks to Mick, pulls out an arrow and makes a single clean cut on his forearm with the tip.

Mick nods to them both to proceed, then looks at me.

"*Come, but hold onto my lead. Do not let go, no matter what we encounter. Do you understand?*"

I nod in agreement and notice a harness appear on Mick's back, and a leash is in my hand. I look at Niamh and Tristan. Fun, carefree smiles have been replaced with looks of riveted attention. At first nothing happens, and then Niamh kneels and blood, dark and red drips into the ground. Tristan does the same. Kneeling they bow their heads.

Niamh is speaking in Gaelic while Tristan is speaking in English.

"Loving Mother Earth, grant us entrance to do your good."

Where Niamh's and Tristan's blood has dropped, iridescent sparkles appear

Tristan and Niamh lean forward. First their hands, then their arms are pressed into the dirt until they are buried past the wounds they have given themselves. They lean down until their lips are almost touching the earth and say quietly...

"We thank you Mother Earth for your wondrous bounty."

The ground vibrates. Between Tristan and Niamh, along the line of iridescent sparkles, where they mixed their blood with the soil, a crack appears in a flash"

A large square of dirt disappears, leaving in its place a stone staircase leading straight down.

Niamh looks over at me, "Be quick."

Mick leads and I follow holding his leash. Tristan nods to Niamh and they also follow. Niamh enters last. She closes the opening.

"Mary is this way," Mick says, pulling me to the right.

Tristan looks at tracks on the dirt floor, "There are others.. We must be quick and quiet."

We travel through a series of ancient dirt tunnels that are almost in total darkness. It is lighter ahead. We enter a large room, filled with boxes covered in dust and cobwebs. I can hear small animals race away as we approach. There are several other tunnels joining ours.

Just as I'm wondering how on earth we will find Mary, Mick sniffs loudly and pulls me into another tunnel. We pass several Fae who are oblivious to our presence. They act like zombies or robots, walking as in a trance.

We turn a corner and come to an alcove, lit by what looks like a floating white Chinese lantern. I don't see any power lines, hmm, wonder how they do that. That's a neat trick.

Then I see a cage, constructed of metal bars. It's only four feet tall and six feet wide. Mary is kneeling on the dirt, wearing a torn sweater and filthy jeans. Her face is covered in dry, caked blood. Her hair hangs in ragged clumps. Her hands are bleeding.

Niamh attempts to open the cage but cannot.

"We are in luck. Full enthrallment has not taken place."

Niamh gives it all she has but cannot open the lock. Tristan tries and fails, then they turn to me.

"Bridget, hold onto the metal and ask it to release."

I stare at Mick and shake my head in denial then look at Mary and see the look of pain on her face. I've got to try. I hold onto the shamrock charm that Molly made for me and do as Mick says. The metal melts away. I kneel before Mary and try to smile.

"Hi Mary, I missed you so much. What are you doing getting into adventures without me," I cry.

Mary looks as if she doesn't know who I am. She has a glassy look in her eyes, like someone on drugs.

"Mick," I cry. "What have they done to her? How can Mary survive magic that is strong enough to take down the Fae? She's only human."

"We can only hope that they ignored her once they realized she was not you. One of the spells Dagda is known for puts his victims into a coma like sleep.

"Mary, will be fine now. Let's get her to safety," Niamh says as she reaches into the cage to help Mary stand. She's weak and shaking. She cries out when she attempts to stand. Niamh and I help her to her feet while Tristan stands guard.

With one of Mary's arms around my shoulders and her other around Niamh, we half carry, half drag her to the tunnel entrance. I'm still holding the lead to Mick's harness in my free hand as Mick goes ahead to make sure the way is clear, and Tristan watches our backs. The going is slow, Niamh stops, and I almost fall under the full dead weight of Mary. Micks' lead has grown longer, and he is several feet ahead of us when a creature materializes immediately in front of Niamh, Mary and me.

"Oh no, an Anthropophagi," Niamh cries.

Tristan rushes in front of us. "Keep going, I have this one."

I can't believe what I'm seeing. The Anthropophagi is a headless creature. His eyes are placed on his shoulders, and his mouth is in the center of his chest. He has no nose.

"Where did he come from?"

Tristan pulls out an arrow and shoots directly into one of the Anthropophagi's eyes. It turns to dust. We rush past the pile of dust and head into the tunnel.

Tristan stands guard at the tunnel entrance next to Mick who stopped when everything happened behind him. Mick looks at Tristan. I can tell that he does not want to leave him.

"You have to get them to safety, I will protect the rear. Get going," commands Tristan.

After I trip the second time, I say, "We need more light."

Two rows of light appear on the ground, like the exit lights on a jet. Hey that is neat. I wonder if Niamh will teach me how to do that.

We hurry as fast as we can to the exit.

Other Anthropophagi appears before Tristan. As he readies his arrow, another creature appears behind him. The creature's face is elongated from chin to forehead. It has four yellow eyes showing from his grey skin. He wraps his four arms around Tristan.

"Move Bridget, Tristan knows what he is doing."

INTERLUDE

Fae War Begins
County Mayo, Ireland

King Padraig and a dozen Fae are fighting. The archers accompanying the King are out-numbered: they choose their shots carefully for Morrigan has sent her creatures, and evil Fae.

Mixed in with this evil, are dozens of their Elders, the be-spelled Fae. The sounds of fighting frighten the young Fae. The King and his team slowly withdraw.

A fledgling Imp runs past, chased by a six foot, ten-armed spider wearing a metal cap. The King backhands his blade, squarely into the spider's chest. The spider turns to dust. Several young Fae panic, run for cover, others dodge flying bat-like creatures as best they can by hiding under low lying branches and wheelbarrows.

Noted for announcing death, Banshees fly overhead, their shrill, screech cutting the air, some of the Fae are frozen in fear.

King Padraig is joined by a few dozen leprechauns. They appear outnumbered. Padraig watches as a young Fae is knocked to the ground. He shouts, "Retreat! Hold fast past the fort."

The King and his crew slowly retreat over the piled rocks, across a field to the base of a small hill.

The goblins shout in triumph, proud that they have beaten the mighty Leprechaun King. A war cry goes up, and they rush forward.

Padraig nods to Shennum. The leprechauns look like ballet dancers as they leap over the hay scattered two feet wide and thirty feet long. They know of the deep trench that they dug underneath the hay. They hide behind rocks. Lying in wait to see their enemies fall into the trench. The trench they have filled with be-spelled oak leaves that will instantly send the invaders into a deep sleep.

More creatures are coming. They swarm the Fae, striking them down. If they get beyond the ditch, Molly's daughter, Evelyn, is prepared. She stands ready with the House Brownies. Following Molly's careful instructions they have concocted a maze of wheelbarrows, old tables, chairs, lamps, coils, of wire and any other item not being used in the castle or barns.

On come the charging goblins, groups that once formed straight lines have to enter into the maze one at a time. Around the first turn they come running and do not notice the trip wire held on either side by a brownie.

Evelyn runs to the fallen goblin and strikes him on the head with her cast iron skillet. As soon as the whack sound is heard, a brownie runs to drag the goblin behind the cart where two others tie him up. Evelyn smiles at her ladies knowing how proud Molly will be of the care they are using in following her instructions.

It begins to rain, obscuring the vision of Morrigan's creatures. Many continue to battle in the mud and in the air, some stop.

King Padraig is using his right hand to wield a sword against be-spelled Fae whom he knows well. With his left hand, he weaves a spell, and with a flash, the be-spelled Fae are wrapped in cord.

"Mick you are needed now!"

Mick materializes next to Padraig. Mick is in full wizard gear, wearing long flowing robes. He is anxious to do what he can to help.

"Yes my lord."

"Mick, create a shield in front of us now."

A tall, red haired leprechaun, stands besides Padraig.

"Shennum, warn the Queen, the South wall has been breached."

Now Padraig holds a sword in each hand. He battles two evil Fae. Mick begins to create a shield. Green sparks fly from his hands. The Fae continue to fight. Three young Fae net one of the flying creatures and put it in a cage. The cage disappears with the creature inside.

A cute young elf is struck down by a giant daddy long legs. The creature raises his leg and prepares to stomp the Fae into the ground. Mick sees this and waves his hand. The Fae disappears from under the creature's leg and materializes next to Padraig, leaving a startled creature holding one foot in the air.

The creature looks around; another Fae shoots him in the butt with an arrow. The creature howls and runs off. Shennum materializes next to Geraldine. "Pardon me my lady. Our outer defense has collapsed."

The strength of her once mortal form shows as she stands and changes from her long, flowing gown to full pirate attire. Geraldine lifts her flaming sword and firmly orders, "Rouse the King and crew!"

"My lady, the King battles at the fort now. He is with my crew. Kearin's crew awaits your orders."

Queen Geraldine arrives at the South Wall of the Fae Kingdom. Kearin is on the ground, battling goblins with a staff. Whack. A goblin turns to dust. She sees the Queen and shouts, "Some are climbing over the wall."

"Geraldine nods to Kearin. She has a sword in one hand and a cutlass in another. She flies to battle bat like creatures. The sound of conflict is all around.

Over the sound of swords clashing a new sound is heard. The ground vibrates.

Kearin stops to stare, a goblin jumps on her back. She throws herself against the wall. The goblin is knocked off. The ground shakes with a thumping noise. The tree limbs move with a swooshing noise. .Dagda sits on the top of the tree cutting and hacking at it with his sickle. A dozen or more creatures ride on the limbs of the tree. Whack he strikes the tree and orders, "Move quickly!"

Kearin cries out, "Your Majesty, look."

With a loud thump, the trees' roots step over the wall and hit the ground with such force that several creatures fall off. With a loud swoosh, the trees' branches swing back and forth.

Geraldine looks up and sees the giant tree carrying several dozen creatures approaching. Creatures fall off with each vigorous swoosh of the branches. She is in shock. Never has she seen the trees abused so badly. She calls out, "Mick, appear!"

"Yes, My Lady?" Mick looks at a tired Geraldine. Her form is fading.

"Mick, please create another shield, we cannot continue."

Mick raises his staff. A green glow creates a large dome, covering the entire castle. The evil Fae trapped inside are quickly turned to dust. The be-spelled Fae are gathered in nets and carried away.

"That is the best I can do my lady. The Goddess grows stronger."

INTERLUDE

Morrigan's Chamber at Old Fort
County Mayo, Ireland

Morrigan sits on a throne of carved stone. Lying on the floor in front of her is Tristan An angry Anthropophagi has his foot on Tristan's back.

"What a bargain, a Leprechaun for a human."

Tristan lifts his face and glares at Morrigan. "It will do you no good. I am too young for your spell to work."

"My friend the Anthropophagi is upset with you and would like you for a snack. Should I oblige him?"

Tristan turns his face to the ground. Dagda stands next to Morrigan.

"We do need a subject to try your new formula, my Goddess." Dagda smiles evilly at Morrigan and she nods agreement.

"Yes, of course. Inject him now, I want to watch."

Tristan struggles. Four jackals and the Anthropophagi hold him down. Dagda injects a long needle into Tristan's arm. Tristan screams in pain.

"No!"

Tristan stumbles forward then crumbles to his knees. He screams again and falls on his back. He stretches out stiff, opens his mouth to scream, and no sound is heard. His hands grip his face and, his green skin turns white. The blue veins and red arteries show clearly. This time his scream is so loud the creatures step back.

"Help...my face... "
Morrigan and Dagda are delighted with the results.

CHAPTER 11

Aunt Molly
Castle, Iona, Scotland

We transport Mary back to the castle. Molly and the other house brownies take charge and send us to the front parlor.

After what seems like hours, Molly enters the room wiping her hands on a towel and looks at me and Mick.

"How is she?"

Molly sits on the couch next to me and holds my hand. "Not to worry dear, we have her cleaned up, and she's sound asleep. She is in no pain."

"How can she be alright after that? What's wrong with her? She didn't say anything?"

"Mary is a strong young lady. Right now she needs food and rest. Please try not to worry dear." Molly turns to Mick, and he explains.

"Bridget, Dagda has placed a spell on her. Similar to what you know of as a coma but she can hear and understand what is being said. As soon as we can we will see what can be done to bring her out of this."

"Aunt Molly there must be something you can give her?"

"Sorry dear, there are no herbs I know of to help bring her back to her old self."

"We must attempt to communicate with Dagda, he would be the best one to break the spell. Otherwise, we may have a long wait."

♣ 101 ♣

I start to cry, and Molly holds me. When I settle down she turns to Mick.

"Is there any word of Tristan?"

Mick lays his head on my lap and I automatically stroke his head, more for my comfort than his. I lay my head against the back of the couch. Mick lifts his head and holds a listening pose. Then looks at me and I yawn.

"Niamh is waiting for Tristan. Go to bed now Bridget. You are sleepy."

I stand as if in a trance and go to the bedroom.

"Mick, why did you do that? You know Bridget wanted to wait up for Tristan's return."

Mick takes his human form, goes to Molly and puts his arms around her. "Tristan will not be returning to us tonight."

Early the next morning I walk into the kitchen and see Molly crying. I rush over to her, "Molly what's the matter, is it Mary. Please tell me is she okay, what's wrong?"

"Mary is the same dear."

She mumbles something that sounds like, "onions." I look at the table. She's peeling potatoes. Something else is wrong. I sit down at the small wooden table, hold her hand and ask, "Please Aunt Molly, tell me what's wrong?"

Just then I hear Simon shouting. Molly jumps to answer him. "We are in the kitchen Simon."

"Molly, please rest I'll take him to Mary. I gave him a little something in his tea last night to help him sleep so he may not be in the best of moods."

Simon rushes in, "Where is Mary? Is she okay? Why isn't she in a hospital?"

"She's okay. Molly took excellent care of her all night and says she will be fine. She's in a coma, but that is only temporary. When she fully recovers she may have some memory lapses, but they will come back eventually." I say a quick prayer that I'm right.

I take Simon to the bedroom that Mary and I shared last night. She's awake and just staring at the ceiling. Thank goodness she is cleaner than when we found her or Simon would have us all shot.

Simon rushes to her side. "What can I do?"

"We are working on getting the cure. For now keep her company. She loves her books."

I grab one and hand it to him. "Read to her and I'll get you some tea." I rush out and close the door to give them some privacy, before I burst into tears. I've got to do something, but what? What good is magic if I can't save my best friend?

I go back downstairs and see Molly still at the table peeling enough potatoes to feed an army.

"Molly, how do I stop Simon from calling in Scotland Yard? He's going to want to find those responsible for hurting Mary."

"Dear, we must tell him the truth, but will he believe it or think we are all crazy."

"I can't tell him the truth, not now, not when he's in this condition."

Peter and Michelle enter the room as I'm explaining to Molly that we can't tell Simon the truth but, I know she's right. It's the only thing to do.

"Bridgette, don't worry. My Pierre will explain everything to Simon."Michelle says as she lovingly looks at Peter and holds onto his arm.

I look over at a stunned Peter and ask, "Do you think you can? He's highly volatile right now."

"He is still struggling with my grand explanation of your magic family. I can try to come up with some story that will hold him for now."

"I thought it over, and Molly is right. It's better if we tell him the whole truth. Even a good story won't work with Simon. He will know we're not being straight with him."

"Bridget, you have other issues to deal with. Michelle and I will take turns sitting with Mary. That will allow Simon time to ferry over and make arrangements to end the search for Mary."

I look over at Molly's red rimmed eyes. Michelle's also looks at Molly and she starts crying.

"Good idea and I'll speak with Simon later. Now please tell me what everyone is upset about, if not Mary."

Molly comes over and sits next to me, starts to say something and starts crying. I hold onto her, and she sobs some more. I can't get her to tell me what is wrong. I've got to get her mind off what is troubling her before she makes herself sick.

"Molly do you have anything for a headache. I seldom get them, but this morning I woke up with the mother of all headaches."

Molly wipes her eyes and says, "Of course dear, I'll whip something up right away."

I watch as Molly leaves. Michelle dries her eyes.

"Okay you guys, out with it, what on earth is going on?"

"Perhaps Mick can explain it better." Peter takes my arm and walks with me to the main hall. I hear voices. They lead to an office, off the main hall that I didn't notice the other day. Mick and Niamh stand before something that looks like a large movie screen, except the image is more lifelike. There is no box holding a screen, just an opening in the wall. It feels as if I could reach into the *screen,* and hug my Greats. Padraig is speaking from Ireland with a dozen faeire, elves and leprechauns nearby. Geraldine stands by his side.

"Quiet now. We all want Tristan back, but we cannot afford to lose anyone else." Padraig says, and then turns to Mick. "Lor..." sees me in the doorway and says, "Good morning my dear, did you sleep well?"

"Good morning your Great. What is this about Tristan, I thought he came home after us last night. Where is he?"

"I am so sorry Bridget. We believe that Morrigan's henchmen captured Tristan at the Abbey and transported him here to the fort. I was just about to ask Mick what he thought was best."

Turning to face Mick, Padraig asks, "Mick, what do you suggest?"

"We will get Tristan out tonight. Many have volunteered, and I thank you. I have chosen Shennum who is close to centurion age."

Several of the Fae begin talking at once. Mick looks over at Niamh who is pacing. *"Now Niamh..."*

"Shennum is just recovering from his round with Morrigan. I am..."

"Sorry Niamh, if I may speak for his Majesty, you are too close to Tristan. You will wait here for us."

Niamh wasn't ready to give in, "Bridget can help, if she goes along, then I could attend to her."

Padraig and Mick exchange a glance but before they can object, Queen Geraldine says, "I agree Niamh, I believe that is an excellent plan."

Mick is silent for awhile then he looks at me. *"I will make the necessary arrangements. We will also transport Simon, Mary, Peter, and Michelle to Molly's cottage. It is a little cozier and should be safe from Morrigan's followers."*

Chapter 12

Fae Kingdom
County Mayo, Ireland

We meet up with Shennum when Niamh, Mick and I teleport to the Fae Kingdom from Iona, and walk quietly along the road to the Fort.

During the day, this is a charming mile long walk, but at night, during a war, it's downright creepy.

I whisper to Mick, "Now I know why I had to take the ferry to Iona. This teleporting long distance is not as easy as it looks."

"I included teleporting in next week's lesson plan."

We walk in silence. "Why don't we teleport directly to where they are holding Tristan?"

"First there is the little problem that the area Morrigan won in battle is shielded. Second, she would expect us to do that and has her creatures prepared."

"Why is there only the four of us?"

"They are on the lookout for us to arrive in large numbers. I thought you were finished with incessant ramblings."

"Not when I'm this nervous." Mick grunts. I turn to Niamh.

"Hey, I don't know how we can get into the fort unnoticed. Do you need to make an opening?"

"Mick will tell you what you need to do. I am only to stand watch out here."

Niamh looks daggers at Mick, still clearly upset, not to play a significant role, in the rescue of Tristan. We reach the back of the fort and Mick stands still.

"The three of you must stay here. Keep alert. I will return shortly."

Mick runs around to the side of the fort. Shennum and Niamh stand with bow and arrow, ready to fire if needed. Niamh turns to Shennum. "Be careful in there."

"Ah away with your blathering now, what harm can she do to me that won't happen in the next few days, no matter what I do?" Shennum's face turns as red as his hair as he blushes from the hug he receives from Niamh.

"I don't like the fact that Mick won't let us go in with him," I complain to them.

Mick comes around the side.

"I found him. Follow me."

We follow Mick to the north side. Look up at a dull light coming from a small slit in the rock. The slit is only large enough for an arrow to pass through.

"Mick, even you won't fit through that opening."

Mick moves next to me, *"I am unable to harm Fae or even someone like Morrigan, but I can give you power when it is needed. Kneel and put your arm around my neck."*

I kneel, and Mick rises up to the opening. I make the mistake of looking down, let a small squeal escape, then close my eyes.

"Hush now. Keep holding on, you are doing extremely well. Okay, you can open your eyes now."

I open my eyes to see that we are three stories up from the ground, close my eyes again and squeeze Mick.

"Loosen up a little, me girl. A dog has got to breathe. You are not afraid of heights. Think of this as a tree limb."

"I'm... not... afraid... of... heights. I've never climbed trees before you teleported me to one. We don't have many trees in Brooklyn and climbing them is probably against the law or something. Okay, we are hovering in the air, now what?"

"Continue holding onto me and raise your right hand and point."

"Like this?" I extend one finger and fold over the rest. My hand looks as if it's a make believe gun.

"Brilliant, now concentrate and draw a door. Where you point, an opening will appear. Keep going until you have an opening large enough for me and Shennum."

I point my hand, with finger extended and a beam of laser light appears from the tip of my finger.

"Hey this is way cool."

Moving along with Mick's help, I cut an opening the shape of a door. Mick lowers me to the ground. Mick and Shennum rise to the opening and go inside.

INTERLUDE

Rescue at the Fort
County Mayo, Ireland

 *Mick takes full human form and tells Shennum, "Go to the right. They have him in the third cell."*

Mick sees two guards approach. He manifests a large black cape that he uses to cloak both himself and Shennum, making them temporarily invisible.

"Hurry, they'll soon see the opening."

Shennum and Mick find Tristan's cell. Shennum is the first through the door and stops. He draws his bow and points it to the man on the floor. Tristan opens his eyes. He appears several years older.

"Put that away. Help me lift him."

"Man, what have they done to you?"

Tristan is having trouble standing. Shennum lifts him over his shoulder. Shennum and Tristan return to the opening in the Castle wall and float down to where Bridget and Niamh stand. Mick returns to dog form and joins them.

CHAPTER 13

Bridget is Shot!
Fort & Castle
Fae Kingdom, Ireland

I point to the opening behind them. "Hurry, we've been spotted."

Mick turns and sees a guard at the opening. *"Bridget, grab hold of my neck."*

Looking at the others he says, *"We will meet up at the cottage."*

Niamh and Shennum carry Tristan between them and dematerialize. Mick and I start to dematerialize just as an arrow is shot, hitting me in the arm.

Mick paces the floor in front of my door. Molly goes out to speak with him and quietly closes the door behind her.

"How is she?"

"She will be fine, no fever, tis but a scratch. You are wearing a hole in the floor. Go on in and sit with her." Mick pushes the door open. I'm tossing and turning on the bed. He jumps up next to me and lays his head on my hand.

"Hush now mo chuisle, all is well."

I look at Mick. His golden eyes look so sad. "Hi Mick, I'd the strangest dream." I stroke Mick's head and he sits up and looks at me.

"Do you feel like talking about it? Sometimes dreams give us some powerful messages."

"I saw my families' graveyard in Ireland. Am I dying?"

"No mo chuisle, you are doing grand."

"Then it means that I need to go there."

I start to get up from the bed, feel woozy and lay back down.

"We'll go as soon as you are well, rest now."

INTERLUDE

Fae Kingdom
Ireland

Mick appears before Padraig, in the Great Hall of the Fae Kingdom in Ireland.

Padraig asks, "How is she?"

"She is fine, but no thanks to me. I never should have allowed her to join us. Since she has come to our aid, she has been stoned, shot by a gun and now an arrow."

"Do you think you had a choice in the matter? You do realize that she is Geraldine's descendent, don't you?"

Queen Geraldine appears next to Padraig. "I heard that dear husband." She turns to Mick. "She will be fine, I just checked on her. It is but a flesh wound. You are not to blame."

Geraldine turns to look at a group of five young Fae speaking quietly at the back of the hall.

"We must put fears to rest. Let us visit Tristan."

The three dematerialize and appear in Tristan's room. Tristan lies on a lounge, seeing them appear, he begins to stand.

Niamh bows to them and says, "Welcome your highnesses, Lord Howth."

They all look at Niamh, puzzled by her formal welcome.

Niamh rushes over and stops Tristan from rising. He smiles at her; she blushes, turns away and leaves the room.

"How are you feeling me lad?"

"I am ready for action your highness."

Tristan starts to rise again, and Padraig signals for him to stay sitting and says, "There will be time enough for battle, rest now."

"Perhaps if you feel up to it, you could join us for a dinner in your honor tonight."

"Of course My Lady, thank you."

"You will be asked to tell of your aging. Tell us a grand story but don't be mucking it up with the truth."

"My Lady?"

Padraig explains, "We need to keep fear away Tristan. Fear is a mind killer. When one wants to defeat a nation the first thing they do is intimidate the people. Drive fear in their hearts and their courage weakens." Mick pauses, "Hmm, now don't you believe that the drug you were given is all they had?"

"Yes, of course My Lord, it is a difficult drug to make. I heard it was the only batch." Tristan winks at Padraig and Geraldine. A little of his boyish charm returning. Padraig touches Tristan on the arm and Geraldine hugs him. They leave, but Mick stays behind and takes a seat next to Tristan.

"How do you feel Tristan?"

"With advanced age I am stronger. I will use my strength to fight their evil even if it is only days before I am old enough to be be-spelled. Perhaps I will be lucky enough to be sent to cathcaruth."

Mick looks at the young man next to him. Gone is the playful youth and in its place, he sees parts of himself. His eyes show anger at not having control at what has been done to him and pain at the harsh memories of what he has endured.

"Yes, you and Shennum are at the same age. Close to the time that she can enslave your mind. What game does she play? Take our youth one at a time or an all out war?"

"I believe it is war. They are ready. They have the numbers. We cannot defeat them."

Mick looks at his young friend, *"With fear, defeat is inevitable. With hope success is assured. Rest now, and remember that our Tristan is a strong, fun loving man. One who does not give anyone the power to frighten him."*

"I don't know if I can face the others," he sighs, *"I need more time."*

"I understand. And I am not telling you what to do. But when you care about people, sometimes you need to give a little thought to what they need. And I think they need you right now."

Tristan lifts his head meets Mick's eyes and blinks.

"They have probably been worried all day."

"Most likely."

Mick leaves Tristan's bedroom and meets Niamh in the hall. They walk off together.

"Will he be okay?" Niamh asks.

"He is okay. Let him rest and continue to love him."

"Love him?"

"You loved him as a young boy. He is still the same, only older. He needs to be treated the same as before. Tell the others."

Niamh looks at Mick, nods and walks off, she returns to Tristan's chamber and stands at the doorway.

"Can I get you anything?"

"Only your company, I have missed you."

Tristan pats the seat next to him. Niamh hesitates then walks over and sits next to Tristan.

"What is it Niamh? Did I do something wrong?"

"Wrong, of course not."

"You haven't called me oaf all day."

Tristan smiles at Niamh. She starts to cry. Tristan puts his arms around her and holds her.

"I was so scared that I would never see you again. I'm still scared. When will this fighting be over?"

"Now, if it was over, who would you be poking with that headpin of yours?"

Niamh laughs with him. "You of course. You oaf."

CHAPTER 14

Molly's Cottage
The Easy Way?

Anxious to be near Mary, I ask Mick to teleport to Aunt Molly's cottage. A gift from the Fae Kingdom, it's located near the old white stone building that held the tenant's cow. Molly's cottage is perfect. It looks like every dream I've ever had of a real home.

Now I know why Mick had me travel by ferry and car to Iona. Teleporting takes a considerable deal of energy. The short distance takes all the strength I have left. I fell asleep as soon as we arrive.

I still feel woozy, but it's exciting to be back in Ireland. I asked Tristan to drive us to the graveyard. I think that was a mistake. I hold onto the dashboard as he narrowly misses an oncoming truck.

"Are you sure you feel up to driving Tristan?"

Mick lies on the backseat with his paws over his eyes and groans.

"I welcome the opportunity."

I stare at how close we are to the edge of the road and close my eyes when we brush against a hedge. My hand automatically goes to hold my magical charm.

"You look very serious me girl, and what is that about now, may I ask."

I open my eyes to see Tristan watching me. "I was remembering when Molly gave me my magical shamrock charm. It's a special gift she wanted me to have before I left for Scotland. If I'd called on it, it might have protected me from the arrow."

"We have a way to go and since my driving is making our friend Mick here nervous, why don't you tell us about it then?"

"I'm still having a hard time believing that I can do magic. I know the Fae can, but it's still hard to believe that I can, you know what I mean?"

"It does take some getting used to when you haven't been practicing from birth." Mick agrees.

"Molly said the same thing, but she also told me that most ancient stories are often based on truths. I know that there are way too many stories of magic to deny its existence. Well, I don't actually deny it but…"

"Bridget we are almost there, tell us about the gift, "Tristan asks.

"After I first visited the mound covering the entrance to the Fae Kingdom, I knew something was different but still didn't believe. Molly gave me this gold shamrock charm to help bring me magic."

I hold it out for Mick and Tristan to see.

"She put it on a chain, so I wouldn't lose it. Then any time I need to call on the family for magic, I just hold onto the clover. I then envision what it is I want, and it will happen."

Tristan smiles, Mick stands up in his seat to look at me.

"Bridget you do know that you are the first child that has been born with all the gifts of your Leprechaun and Faeire heritage."

I nod and touch my shamrock charm.

"We all have some unique abilities. You have more than most, but you have not allowed your gift to surface."

"I was hoping we could continue the training here..."

Just then a bush hits the side of the car. "Please slow down Tristan, oh, turn right there onto that dirt road."

We travel several more unmarked dirt roads, then come to the top of a hill and see a small cemetery holding a dozen graves. Mick and Tristan get out of the car, stand in the sunshine, and check out the surrounding area.

"This is it. I thought it was much bigger. Please stay here you guys, I'll be OK."

I go directly to my families' headstone and kneel. I can hear Tristan ask Mick.

"Has she been here before?"

"Yes their presence gave her strength and courage to help us save the land."

I look at the large black gravestone I saw in my dream. I see not only a long list of those buried overseas but also those family members buried at this spot.

"I have come."

I bow my head and listen, no response. Could I have been wrong? Was there another meaning to my dream?

"Thank you for all that you have done."

I wait a few more minutes and still no response. I start to stand, touch the gravestone and fall back on my heels. I see visions of fighting from the beginning of

Irish history, swords clash, Gaelic shouts and Viking war cries.

Then I hear a female voice. *"As an island, we have always been vulnerable to attacks from outside of our borders and within."*

"Dear family we are at war again. One we must win to protect all of Ireland and the human race. I need your help."

"You are never alone, those that have gone before stand with you."

I wait a few more minutes but just silence and an overwhelming sense of peace. I'm no longer drained from my long trip in the ethers and no longer fear the upcoming war. I say a prayer of thanks, raise my head and stand.

I have to smile at Tristan's comment to Mick, "What happened. She looks taller."

"That is faith. With it, you stand taller."

We return to the cottage and Molly greets us with her purse in hand.

"I have a wee-bit of shopping to do in town. I will be back shortly."

"I'll ride along Aunt Molly, I always enjoy shopping."

"Are you sure you feel up to it dear?"

Molly looks at Mick his ears are up, and he looks alert. Mick looks at Tristan and nods.

"I think that will be a grand idea Molly. Tristan and I are needed at the castle."

They dematerialize before I can join them.

Molly tugs me into the car. "Come on dear, a little shopping trip is just the ticket."

INTERLUDE

Fighting Continues
Fae Kingdom, Ireland

 *Tristan and Mick have been called to battle. They materialize in the commons outside the castle. They look on as Elder be-spelled Fae teleport into the keep with weapons in hand. Younger Fae capture them with large fishing nets.*

"What is happening?"

"A portion of the shield has weakened. I will go to repair it."

Tristan quickly shifts to battle form and sees where a group of Fae is losing ground. He rushes over. An elder dwarf stares at him. He produces a rope and runs around the Elder, tying him up. He gives the rope end to the young Fae to hold.

"That should hold him until we can put him in a holding cell for his safety."

Tristan rushes to the next group. Niamh has captured one of the Elders. There are tears in her eyes. He looks at the other young Fae, they are also sad, "These are their parents. Morrigan breached our shield. She sent them here to cause pandemonium. The real threat will not be far behind." Tristan quickly hugs her and rushes off.

Niamh rushes to where Tristan has been struck down and is not fighting back.

She touches the Elder female Fae who turns to face her. The Elder Fae has tears in her eyes.

Niamh ropes the Elder and turns to Tristan, "Why didn't you fight back?"

"How can I? She's my mom."

Mick finds the opening in the shield and calls on his power, raises his hands and green smoke rises to the opening to form a seal.

CHAPTER 15

Ballina Village
County Mayo, Ireland

Twenty minutes later, Aunt Molly pulls her little car in front of a small grocery store and parks almost between the lines.

What was I thinking? Where's the fun in shopping for groceries? A mall this is not.

"Come along dear."

"That's okay Aunt Molly. I'll wait in the car or maybe sit in the park over there."

Seeing the worried look in my aunt's eyes, I say, "Please, don't worry, I'll be careful."

I hold onto my shamrock charm and smile. Molly shakes her head and carrying her purse and cloth shopping bag, enters the store. I look in the large glass display window and see several ladies greet her. It looks as if this is a traditional, fun gathering place more than a grocer and may take awhile. I smile and leave the car to walk to the little park.

One little bench seat sits on a small patch of grass with the woods as a backdrop. This is a peaceful place, the town planned this spot perfectly. Right near the grocer, so that people could rest before walking back to their homes. Or just sit and watch people walking by. I can hear the birds and very little traffic. I close my eyes and lift my head to the sunshine.

I wonder if there is a bird that sounds like a puppy crying. I look around and don't see any birds or a puppy. I close my eyes, and there's that sound again. That's definitely a puppy crying. I look behind me. It sounds as if it's coming from the woods. Maybe a puppy got tangled.

I take a few steps into the woods when I'm grabbed from behind. Thinking it is a be-spelled Fae I say, "Be gone with ye now."

This guy pulls me around and ties my hands. He is short and muscled, with greasy black hair, and a glazed look in his eyes which tell me that he is human, but under the influence of Morrigan.

"Get a move on and be quiet." He strong arms me through the woods.

"Why are you doing this? Who are you?"

"Quiet!"

He pushes me up the hill behind the buildings on Main Street. I trip over a root. He pulls on my arms. I try to run, but he catches me again. I use my head to push him, but it's like hitting a concrete wall. All I accomplish is getting a headache.

My arm's hurting. I look down at the rope he tied around my wrist. It has come loose. I shake it off and raise my arm to call forth a sword; I raise my other hand to grab hold of my shamrock charm. Before I can reach the charm, the creep grabs my arm and yanks it behind my back.

"Help!"

He pulls my arms tighter and ties both of my arms behind my back. Dang that hurts.

"Mind your manners missy. No one messes with Big Mattie."

"Ow!"

"Keep quiet or I will be giving you a reason to scream."

Mattie pushes me forward, and I fall on cow patties. I try to stand and slip again. I crawl backwards away from him. He laughs. I try to stand and fall against an ancient white oak tree. Then the creep keeps laughing at me, I look down at my new summer outfit. What used to be a bright yellow sundress is now wet, dark brown and stinks? Oh no, not again. I'm covered in cow manure.

"Dear tree please lend me your strength."

Mattie stares at a soft glow that comes from the tree behind me. I move forward to run and break my heel.

"Okay, that does it. Do you know how much I paid for these shoes? You're a jerk. Why don't you guys give up? Morrigan will never get the Fae or the land."

Mattie looks at me with a strange look, but at least he's stopped laughing. He stares at the tree and sees an image of a man emerge from inside the tree. He rubs his eyes, pulls out a gun and points it at the tree then at me.

"With you gone there will be no one left to inherit, it will all be mine," he sneers but the scary intent is lost as his eyes keep darting behind me.

"Is that what she is telling you? Forgetabouit, there is no way she will give anyone the land that the Fae Kingdom is on."

It looks as if he might be listening to me, so I continue to attempt to get through the spell, to the man beneath.

"How can she, or anyone, give you land, we are never *given* land. Our job is to care for the land, to protect it."

I look at the glazed look in his eyes. He's under Morrigan's control in a big way. He just might shoot me. I think of an idea and pray it works. I stare at the gun and concentrate.

"Your gun is on fire."

"What?"

He drops the gun as it explodes into flame. I take off as fast as possible and run uphill. Two creatures with four feet each dart out from behind the trees. I run as fast as I can. They're swinging tree branches at me. I don't look back to see how they do it until one hits me in the butt.

"Hey watch it buddy that hurts."

I come to a small stream. I try to use the flat rocks to get across the stream and sink to my ankles in cow manure.

"Duh, you'd think I'd remember those aren't really rocks."

As I struggle to get out of the huge pile of manure, a giant newt comes up from the stream. I see him and scream. I back away and another newt rises from the stream and grabs my foot. I struggle to get free of the newt and the rope. A Banshee flies low overhead screeching. I close my eyes and concentrate on my tied wrists.

"Rope release!"

Once my arms are free, I lean back on my elbows and use my free foot to kick the newt. My one remaining heel goes in its eye. It turns to dust. I run to the top of the hill. Just as a goblin is about to grab me, it stops like it came up against an invisible wall.

I look around and see an old stone building covered in wisteria and ivy. I see an opening and rush inside. No creature follows. Relieved, I run to a stone bench and sit, gasping for breath.

"I really need to get a spa membership."

The door opens, and Mattie, the creep enters. He looks dazed. He's staring at a space behind me. I turn and see an extremely tall man dressed in a long roman, toga looking, white robe. His hair is black and naturally wild. It even looks as if he has vines and twigs stuck in it. It's in a pony tail, held back with a vine.

I look at the robe and think of Friar Xavier from England. This must be one strange local monastery. He does look a little rough, but Friar Xavier was an enormous help, maybe this one will be also.

"Come with me," snarls Mattie still looking wild eyed at the Friar.

I stand. My mind is going a mile a minute.

How can I make a run for it when he's blocking the door?

I frantically look around for another exit. Then the ghost disappears, and Mattie moves closer. All of a sudden the Friar is standing between Mattie and me. I sit back down to watch Mattie's reaction. I'm kind of used to ghosts. But to see them materialize from thin air the first time, would take one's breath away. The creep sees the ghost take shape in front of him.

"Go Away. HELP!"

Mattie backs up, runs away. The spirit gives chase, flying inches from Mattie's back. He ducks inside an old discarded confessional. The ghost moves the screen separating the two sections.

"Do you care to confess?" Says the ghost of a Friar whose eyes glow red.

"HELP!"

Mattie leaves the confessional and runs. The ghost is in front of him. Mattie falls and hits his head on the corner of a stone fountain. The ghost floats over him. Mattie's still breathing. Then the ghost floats over to where I'm sitting.

"Thank you for your help."

"Not a problem at all, enthralled humans are not allowed in here."

"Enthralled? Like be-spelled, under someone's influence? Yeah, he's enthralled alright."

"Hi, I'm Bridget," I say as I extend my hand.

"I am called Fergus. I protect these hallowed grounds... You can see me?"

Fergus floats above me, and I have to tip my head way back to follow him.

"Of course, I can see you, shouldn't I?"

"Not unless I allow it as I did for that young man there. No one has willingly seen or spoken with me for an extraordinarily long time."

As he is speaking, his form becomes more solid. He sits next to me.

"Let me introduce myself, I am Fergus, born here in County Mayo"

"I'm so happy that you were here to help me... ah.., why are you here?"

"To protect what is ours. Even in your written history, since 431, when Pope Celestine I, sent his clerics to guard this area, we have been on guard."

As he speaks of his role, he pulls back his shoulders and looks regal. For someone with twigs in his hair, that is saying something.

"To whom did you say I have the pleasure of speaking with?"

"Oh, I'm sorry, my name is Bridget Carins. I'm from Brooklyn, New York. I'm very pleased to meet you."

I learned my lesson with Friar Xavier. On second thought, I'm not keen to shake hands with a ghost, so I just nod.

"You are not going to run from my...shall we say.., limited presence?"

"I'm surprised to meet a live ghost here in Ireland, well not live," I laugh, "but after meeting my Fae family in Ireland and the spirit of a Friar in London, nothing surprises me."

"Have you been enjoying your visit?"

"It has been exciting, I..."

I hear Aunt Molly. She sounds scared, *"Bridget, where are you?"*

"We're at the top of the hill. Could you drive up to get me? I think I'm behind the church. I look a wreck."

"Who is with you?"

"I met an Irish Friar. He helped me get away from..."

"Hold on, I will be right there," Molly says.

I jump up and head for the door.

"Must you leave? I have a great many questions."

"Yes. I'm sorry. I forgot I can mind-speak. I should've spoken with my aunt earlier. She sounds very upset. Would you like to come with us? She would love to meet you."

"Are you sure?"

"I'm positive. Her only problem will be trying to figure out how to feed you. Will the Fae be able to see you?"

"I choose those who can see me. You have a gift. I did not choose to show myself to you and yet you see me. I may choose to show myself to others."

I smile at the holy friar; he must be one of those hermit guys, the kind that does not like to be around people. We walk to the door, and I point to Mattie.

"What about him?"

"He will sleep for a few hours. He is a decent man when not be-spelled. The Father in charge of this parish will attend to his care."

We race towards Molly's cottage at breakneck speed. I put my head out the window to speak with Molly

"Don't you think its dangerous driving with your head out the window?"

"The smell is worse than the last time you had a run-in with cow dung."

"Oh, so that is why you're driving so fast. Sorry about that."

"I have a little trouble seeing, since the smell of ye brings tears to my eyes."

"Ah I'm sorry. I thought sitting in the back seat would help. The Friar doesn't seem to be too bothered by the smell."

Fergus sits in the front seat with both hands on the dashboard.

Molly looks over at the frightened Fergus.

"It's me driving that is brothering him, he isn't one to worry about natural smells."

"Why can't you zap me back to the cottage?"

"I am a House Brownie. I can only use my magic if I am in the house. I can return to it if I originated from it, but we drove to town."

"Mick is going to be mad that I forgot to use magic to protect myself."

"You are okay now, that is what counts."

I sit next to Molly on the couch smelling like fresh lavender. Fergus is hovering, taking in all of the interesting items around him. I don't think one book title on the wall of floor to ceiling books missed his inspection. I can tell he is enjoying himself. I let out a little yelp as Mick materializes in front of me.

"We need to talk."

He sounds grumpy. He looks over at Fergus and nods.

"Somehow I thought you would want to talk. Let's go for a walk," I say as I grab a sweater from the hook by the door.

The flower garden smells fantastic. Little floating lights lead the way to a bench near a pond. I sit and relax, listening to the frogs sing. Mick jumps up beside me.

"Going off by yourself was foolish."

"You're right. I didn't think."

"Want to talk about it?"

"I guess."

Mick nudges my hand, encouraging me to get on with it.

"I was scared, Mick. I forgot everything you taught me. Heck, I even forgot I could mind-speak."

I put my arm around Mick's neck. "With my arms tied, I couldn't touch my shamrock charm..."

"Did you do any magic that you were not trained to do without touching it?"

"I can't I... wait, I did. When my arms were behind my back and ... I didn't touch my charm, but how?"

"You have been born with your gifts. They are your birthright. You don't need outside things to connect you to your magic."

"Why did Aunt...?"

"Your aunt wanted you to find your confidence. Sometimes it is easier for us to believe in things outside of ourselves, rather than believe in ourselves."

Mick lies against me. His strong, warm body feels so comforting, like a strong human hug. We sit in silence enjoying each other's company until Mick sniffs my hair and starts sneezing. I explain about falling in the cow patties and Aunt Molly having me bathe in her special bath soap.

Then Mick starts his strange hacking laugh, and I join in. I laugh so hard that the tears come. With the release of tears and laughter, I'm finally able to relax.

INTERLUDE

A Dryad Named Fergus
County Mayo, Ireland.

Molly looks at Fergus, *"Dear Guardian, my niece Bridget introduced you as Friar Fergus. May I ask why have you not told her who you are?"*

"In time."

"I have never heard of a Dryad of your power rising before. Are you here to help us?"

"To observe."

Fergus sits next to Molly on the couch.

"Tell me of Bridget."

"She comes from a large city in America."

"Show me what you know of this place." Fergus touches Molly's head and images of inner city Brooklyn present themselves to him; burned out cars on the street, gang graffiti, tenements, police sirens, smog. Fergus pulls his hand away and soars to the ceiling.

"What is this? What have they done? Where are the trees?"

"They are in a park for some to visit. It is the same in many places now."

"HER anger is showing throughout the world... Now I know why."

"Our Queen and King are worried it will be the same here."

"Never!" And with that shout Fergus disappears. Molly smiles and does a little happy dance around the room.

CHAPTER 16

Moonlight
County Mayo, Ireland

We watch the moon and stars and listen to the sounds of the night. No city lights to interfere with millions of stars overhead. Funny how even those little floating lights that lit our way to the bench, are no longer lit.

"Soon encounters, as you had today will be a thing of the past. Soak in the beauty of the night. Let it fill you, strengthen you."

Mick has his head on my lap and we just sit looking at the night sky. I can't remember when I felt so happy and content.

Funny after the day I've had, I can let out a sigh of contentment.

"Remember the formula. First you have the negative drain away with the help of God's gifts. Second, let's speak of a positive thing."

"Yes, the formula. Lesson number five thousand and twenty two." I laugh.

"At the gravesite, I was reminded that my ancestors are always with me."

"Awareness that we are a part of those who have gone before, gives us strength."

"I remembered you said that before. Funny how I need to be reminded, why is it that we often forget the good stuff."

We sit quietly for a few minutes.

"Their life was hard. When I first came here, I had visions of what our ancestors have gone through. They worked extremely hard to save this land for us. Today it was not just visions of my ancestors but all the warriors in the British Isles."

"The hope is that each generation will have it easier than the last."

"You're great Mick, I can talk to you about anything and you don't laugh at me."

We all have our challenges to overcome. It is what makes us strong."

I hug him tight and say, "I wish I could meet a guy as nice as you Mick."

I nuzzle Mick's neck and hear him make a rumbling sound. If I wasn't so sure he's a dog, I would swear he was purring.

INTERLUDE

Mick Cares
Kings Chamber
Fae Kingdom, County Mayo, Ireland

Padraig is dressing in full fighting gear. Forest green body suit, brown leather vest. Mick is pacing.

"Mick my boy, you worry too much. Bridget will be able to stop Morrigan. You must believe this. You, most of all, must believe that she can do this."

"I have come to care for her. I do not wish to see her harmed."

"Do not allow thoughts of failure to enter your mind. You must begin to imagine, as we are, her total success."

Padraig watches his long time friend as he paces the floor. I can tell you care for her. I am certain that Bridget also has deep feelings for you..."

Mick stops pacing and looks at Padraig. "She loves a dog!" He changes into dog form and says, "I need to prepare her for battle."

INTERLUDE

Morrigan's Chamber
Fort
Fae Kingdom, Ireland

In the black stone fort on the Fae land, Morrigan and Dagda watch the vision of Bridget as she sits with Mick.

"I am sorely disappointed Dagda. My orders were to capture Bridget. One young human girl and you and your team cannot detain her?"

"She will be yours My Goddess. She will face many of your followers. My plan is to tire her. You, my Goddess will strike the killing blow.

"You know I prefer not to kill humans directly."

Dagda moves to a life size stone statue in Morrigan's collection.

Morrigan turns to Dagda and looks at the green Connemara marble of Elf.

"How smart you are dear Dagda. I will enjoy seeing the look on my cousin's face when I show her the newest addition to my collection. Ah, it has been entertaining to watch my cousin suffer. Oh well, let us finish this."

CHAPTER 17

Battle for the Fae Kingdom
County Mayo, Ireland

Padraig stares grimly as hundreds of Fae appear. Some are familiar once friendly faces now spellbound. Many are evil Fae, creatures and ghouls of every size and shape created by Morrigan, to do her biding.

"Here they are my dear, after all these years, this struggle will soon be over."

Padraig has a sword in each hand. Queen Geraldine stands by his side, dressed in pirate attire, cutlass in one hand, sword in another. Mick and I stand beside them.

Mick asks, *"How may I assist, your Majesties?"*

I look around me. Wow, suddenly the Fae War is all too real and I'm in the middle of it!

Padraig does not hesitate and answers, "Ah, perhaps a diversion or two, my dear friend."

"Yes my Lord."

Mick changes into a whirlwind. Steps between a goblin and a budding Fae, trips another four legged Fae. Knocks one giant Anthropophagi against three goblins, they fight among themselves.

A pixie ties the boots of two giants together. They fall and cannot get back up. Laughing at the scene, Mick spots Aillen Mac Midhna. The dreaded Aillen puts his victims in a trance and then burns them with his flame. He has a dwarf and a pixie in a trance. They look as if they are sleeping peacefully. Mick changes to a mystical Phoenix rushes over and covers them with his wings just as Aillen shoots a burst of fire at the young Fae. The flame spatters into nothingness.

Mick looks above Aillen's head and sees a large cauldron of oil. With a wave of his hand, he sends fire above and the oil explodes circling Aillen. Shennum shoots an arrow and Aillen turns to dust. Mick looks around, sees me staring at him and bows his bird head.

I watch as Tristan battles a goblin. They wrestle. The goblin magically produces a staff to strike Tristan. Tristan produces a sword and cuts the staff into several pieces. The goblin produces a jug of oil. It hovers in the air, and then empties on Tristan's head. Tristan shakes himself clean and produces a pot of gold that swings at the goblins head, and knocks him out.

Still dazed by seeing Mick change forms, I see a two headed troll come rushing towards me. After a split second to consider, I concentrate and create a sword. Fergus appears at my side.

"Would you care for a little assistance?"

I push the sword into the troll's eye, and it turns to dust. An anthropoid takes its place. I pretend to give up the fight but change my sword into a whip, and wrap it around all four of the anthropoids' arms and tie him up like a pretzel.

"I would love a lot of assistance. An Army would help."

I study the battle, trying to get a perspective on what is happening around me.

Then I hear, *"Those who have gone before stand with you."* I see my dream of thousands of headstones.

I go to where Queen Geraldine and King Padraig are surrounded, a rat like creature blocks my way. I create a flaming sword and fight with it as I say to Fergus who is floating next to me.

"Fergus, Ireland has many fallen warriors... could you get them to help us?"

"I do know of one who can grant that request. Come. We will see what can be done."

I finally get the rat creature. It turns to dust. Fergus takes my hand, and we dematerialize leaving the sound of wings and war behind.

When I open my eyes I'm only a little nauseous, I must be getting use to this teleporting thing.

"I know this place. We're at Croagh Patrick Mountain.

We kneel at the base of the mountain. With our heads bowed we pray.

Then Fergus stands and calls out, "Oh Holy Mother Earth, I, your humble servant beg a moment of your time."

The mountain in front of Fergus is dark and quiet. Then a rock falls and another. A wave of ground shivers.

"Your children struggle to protect you. They need your help. For this night, we beg you to release your warriors for one last battle."

The mountain is still, then shivers and glows.

I stand and call out, "Your Fae love and protect you. They only wish to continue to honor you."

I watch for a sign that she has heard. When nothing more happens I say, "Holy mother earth. Many humans also honor and protect you. They are small in number but growing daily. Please help us this night."

The ground begins to shake and right in front of us an opening appears. Fergus nods at me, takes my hand, and we fly to a graveyard outside some ancient Castle ruin.

Fergus stands in front of a stone that lies flat in the ground. "It is for you to ask, my child."

Why did I ever watch those zombie movies? Why am I here, this is crazy. Before I give into my fears, I remember what's happening on my land, on the land of my ancestors, at the source of all Fae power in the world. Okay overcome your fears and just do it!

I shout, "Come forth, there is work to be done."

I can't help it. I crack up with hysterical laughing. I'm beginning to sound like a cartoon version of *Sabrina the Witch.* I look over at a puzzled looking Fergus and laugh some more until the ancient gravestone moves. Clumps of dirt fall away as the stone moves. An opening appears to reveal a stone casket. An unusual rock sits on the casket.

Why a rock on top of a casket? Is this someone that they want to stay buried? Okay, what am I doing? Who is Fergus anyway? Maybe I just unearthed an evil vampire. The stone makes an unearthly sound as it slides from the top of a stone slab. The slab moves, making an extremely loud screeching sound.

I stare at the stone. It's black, cone-shaped with needle-like etchings embedded on the surface in what looks like gold. Then I remember when all this began. The little people were holding hands and moving around a stone. This stone! I knew it looked familiar. I'd seen a drawing of it in the Brooklyn Museum. An ancient pagan worshipping stone, people used it to call upon help with the harvest. Later they used it to call a warrior to aid them.

A skeleton hand emerges holding the remnants of a badly rusted sword. The skeleton stands, dropping all sorts of bugs. Yikes, I turn to run, and Fergus takes my hand.

"Let me introduce you my child."

I look at the skeleton as skin starts showing, eye balls, and hair take form.

"Bridget, may I introduce Brian Bóroimhe, or you may know him as Brian Boru. In, 1011 all of the regional rulers in Ireland acknowledged Brian's authority. He was often called, Imperator Scottorum, or Emperor of the Irish. He will lead your army."

I am so grateful for the glacial cold of Fergus's hand. Otherwise, I think I would embarrass myself and pass out. With my luck lately, I would fall head first into the casket.

I open my eyes and see a hunk clad in full regalia. He wears a crown and carries a shield with three lions painted on it. His sword looks deadly.

He smiles at me. Picks up my hand and kisses it. Yuck. Then he winks. Yikes! He's flirting! Mary is so not going to believe this.

"Ah, pleased to meet you your Kingship. Ah...bye, got to go raise my army..."

Finally, my head gets the message to my feet, and I run out of that graveyard with hundreds of more stones moving, releasing their occupants. I think the screeching sound of stone slabs moving will haunt my dreams forever. It's as though my running past them is moving them along quicker. I can't help but notice dozens of skeletons take shape in front of me. Can you say serious horror movie here? Yuck.

Okay take a deep breath.

I turn around and yell above the screeching noise, "The Fae Kingdom needs you. Please go help them."

Brian Boru and his army of still forming skeletons begin their march to the Fae Kingdom, as they walk past fields I see foot soldiers rise from the bog, carrying a variety of weapons.

We teleport to Scotland but by now I am running on empty. "Hey Fergus, we need many more, but flying drains my energy. Do you think if I put myself in a state of conscious hypnosis to totally relax, you could teleport us to England and I can preserve my energy for the battle to come? Mick has been teaching me how to do this to relax and I've become pretty good at it."

"I too am concerned about your waning energy levels as we continue to fly. I think your idea has merit and certainly is worth a try. But first if we could get help releasing the earth's occupants in the rest of the land, we would have many more warriors for our cause. Perhaps Mother Earth will grant us yet another favor to help end this nightmare that is all of Morrigan's making! I think I know of a way to accomplish our goal before we teleport back to the Kingdom. Will you put your trust in me Bridget?"

"Fergus, you have so far saved my life and impressed Mother Earth to yield up her dead for our cause just this one night. What's not to trust!"

"Then kneel my child, and pray again as though your very life depends upon it!"

As I close my eyes I see Fergus stand tall with his arms wide. He calls out once again to Holy Mother Earth for an audience with her. I'm startled by her immediate response, no delay here, the ground is shaking but I don't dare open my eyes for fear of hexing the line of communication that Fergus seems to have with the powers that be. Suddenly, I'm stunned by a warm, rich, commanding female voice echoing in my mind, responding to Fergus's call. Eavesdropping is not one of my faults but for crying out loud, what choice do I have here!

"You summon me again Dryad. Have I not honored your request for warriors to rise up from their slumber this night and fight for the Fae?"

"Yes, O Holy One, and I am eternally grateful for your kindness to one as lowly as myself in granting my request."

"Your humility appeals to me Guardian. Put forth your petition then, as there is unrest like an evil shadow creeping across the land even as we speak."

"My young steward, Bridget, being but a frail human, has the iron will to succeed but her body grows weary as she calls the specters forth to fight in battle. It has long been foretold in Fae lore that she is the 'One' who will have a pivotal role in the destruction of Morrigan and her minions, but she needs to maintain her strength for that destiny. Oh Great Giver of Life, would you direct emissaries to go forth in her stead, to summon the ghosts of ages past for our cause?"

"Sentinel of the Innocent, you do much for one who was sent merely to observe. But I am encouraged by your interest and willingness to become involved in the affairs of the beings that inhabit my lands. Therefore, I will grant your request. The Wind Spirits, who rustle your boughs in the canopy of the forests, will be your emissaries. They will fly swiftly on the mighty winds of the heavens over all of Ireland, Scotland and England, calling the fallen heroes to rise once again and fight for the Just and Good folk of the Fae Kingdom."

"Thank you My Mother for your generous provision for Bridget's time of need. We will now fly to the Kingdom to face the path Destiny is calling us to."

"Godspeed on your journey my valiant Dryad, I now take my rest until the sun brings a new dawn."

With that the earth shudders again and my eyes fly open as I pitch forward, flat on my face from my prayer position. Just adding a little grass stain on my clothes, whose going to notice with the all the dirt from the graveyards. Will I ever be graceful? Guess that's a question that will have to wait. Fergus and I have to be on our way. Wait till I tell Mary what's happened. She's going to have me committed in the loony bin for sure!

♣♣♣

The Wind Spirits undulate as in a well choreographed dance, riding the currents Mother Earth put into motion. They are carried over Scotland all the while singing their song to those long ago put to rest, compelling them to once more rise to the challenge put before them. As we make our way back we fly over several castle ruins. As we watch, the earth moves, releasing its occupants. Stone slabs move all over Scotland.

"Who are these guys Friar?"

"Roibert a Briuis or Robert the Bruce, at one time he was the future King of Scots. William Wallace has been called the liberator and creator of Scotland. No worry dear, they both are acutely familiar with the battlefield."

"I'm glad Friar Xavier and Skeletor were also available. They will direct them to action. That sure was a funny reaction from Friar Xavier when I introduced you. What's up with that, was it a miscommunication via mind-speak?"

"I am not a Friar my child. It was easier to let you believe that rather than explain at the time. You see I am a Dryad. There are many misconceptions about us. I am the spirit of the trees, at times a Druid of old. Mainly, as you have seen, I am a protector and supplicant to our Mother Earth."

"Whatever title, I could never have done this without your help. Thank you so much. I was very afraid that I would not have the energy to make it to England."

"Why is that my dear?"

"I believe Morrigan will try to hit the Fae all at once from every country she is active in. I can't get home to the States or even to Europe, but who do we contact in England?

"What a wonderful experience my child, I am pleased that my friend Anselm was of some assistance."

"Thank you... ah, Fergus, your friend Anselm was a terrific help. We don't have much time but with his help and that of Lord Nelson and the Duke of Wellington we got the guys out in force. Florence has a lot of pull with Queen Boadicea and Lady Godiva, they will see that the ladies get to the correct spots."

"If not, then Winston is extremely capable of leading the charge."

"Wow, this mind-speak with spirits sure beats any social networking I've ever heard of, glad you thought of it."

I hear a strange rattle and grin like an idiot. I think I got the old Dryad to smile.

The night is filled with the sound of stone sliding against stone. To put my mind at rest, Fergus opens a portal and I see the vision of an army of skeletons takes shape, along with spears, swords, shields, axes, bows and slings. Once complete my skeleton army flies up and joins others on the flight to Stonehenge to save the young Fae. Now I can return to Ireland knowing that I've done my best to remove Morrigan's evil influence over the British Isles, now to free Ireland of her for once and for all.

CHAPTER 18

Return to
The Fae Kingdom.

We return to the Kingdom, landing in the midst of the battle taking place on the Commons. A Banshee is flying over the heads of those battling below. I rush into the center of the fighting and create a spear on the run. Boy I'm getting good at this.

A Banshee is ready to grab Shennum. I hurl my spear towards it. She laughs at my poor attempt. The Banshee continues to laugh until the spear turns into a giant serpent and swallows her.

I see Niamh in full fighting form, her blue iridescent skin and silver blue wings are spread open as she flies over yet another Aillen Mac Midhna who's playing his harp to a group of brownies. The brownies are falling to the floor. Niamh grabs the harp from a fallen Aillen and smashes it over his head. He gets angry, shoots flame and singes Niamh's wing. Niamh falls to the ground. As Aillen is shooting the flame Tristan shoots an arrow into Aillen's foot. He looks at his foot while still shooting flame, sets his own foot on fire. Tristan rushes to Niamh's side. She is shaken up but unhurt.

I hear a cry. A spear has struck the King. He is lying on the floor, Shennum and Geraldine rush to his side.

Padraig shouts, "Shennum remove this, we have a battle to win."

"Right away your Majesty."

Queen Geraldine kneels by his side, "Hush mo chuisle. Lay still for a moment."

Shennum pulls the spear free.

Geraldine leans over Padraig and uses the last of her power to close the wound in her husband's shoulder. She fades. She is at full transparency. She has no power left to fight.

While I'm watching to make sure the Great's are okay, Morrigan's followers surround me. Tristan and Niamh swing in on vines. The two stand back to back with me.

INTERLUDE

Outer Wall Defense
Fae Kingdom, Ireland

Molly and a dozen house faeire are guarding the wall. They pour honey and flour on the heads of the giant newts and swat at the flying bats with brooms.

Two brownies hide until they get a signal from Molly, jump up and capture several flying squirrels in a bed sheet.

One brownie uses a frying pan to hit a goblin as she sits on his shoulders.

Molly watches the action, holding tight to her broom. Behind her a duck-like creature rises and knocks her to the ground.

CHAPTER 19

The Dead Arise Across The British Isles

I look up to see rank upon rank of warriors fly into the kingdom. Niamh shouts, "More? No. It can't be."

I see warriors still in transition from spectral form. Rusting weapons and tattered banners are taking shape as I watch. Some are wearing very little. Some appear to be wearing dirty blankets held in place with a large pin. A group of fierce looking fighters materialize behind the group closing in on me and quickly turn the evil Fae to dust.

Fergus appears at my side. "Let me introduce you to Cúchulainn. At the age of seventeen he defended Ulster single-handedly against the armies of queen Medb of Connacht in the epic *Táin Bó Cúailnge*."

I stare open-mouthed. Cúchulainn, has three colors of long curling hair that flows down his back. Next to his skin the hair is brown, in the middle it is red; on the outside, it's gold. Around his neck are a hundred tiny links of jewels, his hands and feet are hawk's talons and hedgehog's claws.

Cúchulainn takes on a dozen villains of various shapes and sizes. They turn to dust.

"I'm so happy he's on our side. Who are they?" I point to the right as more men and women appear.

Fergus smiles, "The Fianna."

"What are they yelling?"

"Diord Fionn. It is the war-cry of the Fianna. They frequently employ its use prior to and during battle to put fear into their enemies."

Tristan almost drops his sword as a hundred fierce Fianna materializes, carrying swords and spears. They make quick work of Morrigan's creatures in their vicinity.

I look at the tall man taking command. "Who is that man?"

"Brian Boru of course he looks a little different from the last time you met him. You could never keep him away from a fight to rid Ireland of evil."

I continue to watch the fighting. I back up and get out of the way, lean against a tree. Watch as the Fae youth capture their Elders in nets. One by one the evil Fae turn to dust.

An arm grabs me from behind. "Tell your spirit army to stop." A man in a business suit holds a sickle blade to my neck.

"You've got to be kidding me, no way. I will not stop. We are winning."

He holds me tighter, and I feel the blade cut into my neck. A hot, sticky trickle of blood runs down my blouse.

"Listen buddy, you're a businessman. You know how this will end. We have Mother Earth on our side. Morrigan might as well throw in the flag."

His pressure on the blade lightens on my skin. "Keep talking."

"I worked for a real estate magnet named Hoffman. He's a billionaire. He has an office in the Empire State building. He's a big shot. I know that I can get you a position as his top guy and soon you will make millions, if not billions."

"How can you guarantee he will hire me to such a lofty position?"

"I worked for his mistress. Most of the money is in his wife's name. You could blackmail him with the information I have. I promise you."

"What do you want?"

"You are the only one who can bring Mary out of her coma."

"How then do I get Morrigan to believe that you got away from me?"

I thought about it for awhile then ask, "Dear tree, can you hear me? Please knock Dagda down and pretend that you are killing him by stepping on him. Please don't kill him, he is going to help my friend Mary and I need him."

I hear Fergus shout, "Stop warriors of Ireland."

All stand still. Frozen in place at Fergus's command, all eyes are on me, and Dagda, Morrigan's right hand man.

As if thinking of her brings evil fortune, she materializes directly in front of me. I feel a sense of menacing power. Icy fingers walk across my spine as I remember the lady in the caves under the fort. Her eyes stare with a chilling intensity.

With the unmistakable edge of anger in her voice she says, "You child, have interfered where you are not wanted. It ends now."

She turns to Dagda, "Good work Dagda."

I cry out, "Don't stop fighting... OW!"

Dagda tightens his hold. I struggle and remember to use my magic but somehow his hold diminishes any abilities I have. I remember my self-defense classes and slam my head back as far, and as fast as I can.

I knock Dagda back a step. The tree reaches down and knocks him on his back then steps forward and stands on him. I can see his hand move as he tries to struggle free, the tree holds on tight. I imagine he is a little uncomfortable right now.

I hear a low rumbling sound in my head, "You will never use us to do your bidding again."

"I promise," squeaks Dagda."

Morrigan raises her staff, a black light is headed for me, and I'm stuck like a deer in headlights.

I hear Mick shout, "Get down!"

I drop to the ground.

A Gryphon wraps me in his wings, and then transforms his wings to thousands of mirrors. In a split second a black beam hits the mirrors and boomerangs back to Morrigan.

Little by little Morrigan turns to stone. The Gryphon falls. I pick up his head and cry. I hold him in my arms. I look down and see that the beautiful feathered head of an Eagle is now a very handsome man.

What can I do? I hold on as tight as I can and holler, "Someone get an ambulance!"

I guess my shouting shocks him out of it. He recovers and looks at me with the same handsome features I danced with in England. With the same loving, sensitive, amber shaded eyes I've grown used to these past few months, my Mick.

"Who? Why?" I stand up quickly. Confused and bleeding, I stagger back. Molly rushes to me. Mick lifts me up and takes me to my room.

♣♣♣

I wake a little dazed. Molly sits in a chair by my side.

"What happened?"

"You fainted dear."

"Nobody faints in real life that's just in romance novels. Is everyone okay?"

"They are thanks to you. Now drink this, it will rebuild the blood you lost."

I hold the steaming brew in my hands and drink as instructed. Still a little in shock, I ask, "It's over?"

"Yes, peace has come to the Fae at long last."

"Mary..."

"Dagda did as you requested. Mary is awake and asking for you. Dagda wants information on a Mr. Hoffman?"

"I'll write it down now. Please give it to him so he can leave right away. I don't think he has many friends here."

I wrote down the contact information for Mr. Hoffman's mistress. She had been more than willing to tell me what a creep he was when I delivered her monthly cash. I'm sure she will love the attention of a man to tell her troubles to. I fold the paper and hand it to Molly.

"Now be sure to finish up."

I should be happy, but somehow I'm sad. I guess they don't need me anymore. Neither does Mary. Now I'm all alone. I drink from the cup Molly offers, lie down and fall asleep.

Mick walks in, a green flash appears, and he holds a blanket. He covers me with it and strokes my cheek. I feel as if I'm asleep but aware. I know that he sits in a chair next to the bed. I feel my friend's presence, my Mick.

CHAPTER 20

A Fun Awakening
Fae Kingdom, Ireland

I wake the next morning to the pleasant sound of a dozen faeire tittering laughter. I see Molly creating beautiful garments and putting it in gift boxes.

"Where did all of this come from?" I look around at the large array of boxes. This is just like my ball at Buckingham Palace. Are we having a party?"

"One of my latest gifts from our ancestors is that I can conjure up a wardrobe fit for a princess," says a smiling Molly.

"They are gifts from your family and friends. We are to help you prepare for the celebration ball. Would you like to open them?" Kearin asks, anxious to see the garments.

"Are they all for me?" I jump out of bed and begin to open the boxes. In the first box, I find a pair of Jimmy Choo's embossed with Swarovski crystals.

"I've never seen anything like these. They are beautiful."

"As they should be for they were made by the fellows up North," Natalie says.

Two more faeire fly in and have a large box between them. I open it and hold up an elegant evening gown.

"Do you like it?" There is another dress and under things from Michelle's family in France, says my old friend, Que-tip.

"I can't believe anything could be so beautiful." I dance around, holding the evening gown of pure silk, in pastel rainbow colors. The fabric feels fantastic. A band of sparking crystals gives it that heavenly bling.

"I can't believe that all of this is for me!" I hold the dress up and look at myself in the mirror. The happy faeire dance alongside. Que-tip flies over and hovers in front of me. She puts her hands on her hips and asks, "And who else may I ask saved the entire Fae race!

"Oh Que-tip, I missed you so much. How was the battle in England?"

"It was horrible. We all feared the worst until those scary looking blokes showed up. You could have warned a person you know. Like near gave me the flutters seeing skeletons, yuck!"

Que-tip holds up the slip and dances with it, Niamh dances with my shoes.

"I'll be back and check on you, but I must be off and conjure up gowns for Mary and Michelle. This is so much fun," Molly waves and disappears.

I look at Niamh, "Those shoes are a work of art."

"They are from Salcraig in the Boarders of Scotland. Some of the elder leprechauns still hold a good trade there in making shoes." Niamh says. There goes my belief that leprechauns are just found in Ireland. Harmony puts a hat on my head and still holding the dress, we dance and twirl. I love to hear their carefree laughter. Niamh and Que-tip drop down exhausted.

"They are delightful gifts for you to wear at the celebration ball and long after. We are happy you like them." I stop and look at Niamh.

"I can't."

Niamh looks at Que-tip. The faeire pick up the empty boxes and paper and leave. I sit down on the bed.

"What's wrong Bridget?"

"I can't go."

"And why not may I ask?"

"I can't face him."

"Ah, Tis Lord Howth that has you in this state?"

"Oh no, that's right, he's a Lord?" I cover my face and groan.

"I told him everything. I thought he was a dog. I rolled in the grass with him."

"It was grand to see you both having such fun."

I jump up. "Oh no, I accused him of smelling my butt!" Niamh busies herself with hanging up my gown, but I can see her shoulders shake with laughter. I plop back on the bed and bury my face under the pillow.

"What was that he turned into to save me?"

"A Gryphon. The Gryphon has the head of an Eagle, and the body of a lion. It ruled both air and land. They are watchful, loyal, strong and swift. In ancient times, they were symbols of guardianship, protection and the retribution of justice."

"If Mick could shift into anything, why did he choose a dog form?"

"Their Majesties," Niamh said as if that explained all.

"He's not Fae why does he have to do what they ask?"

"Tis a long story but one you need to hear."

Niamh sits in the chair next to the bed. I prop myself up with pillows.

"In 1574 Grace O'Malley had a run-in with the Earl of Howth. She had Mick kidnapped. To get him returned his father had to promise that the doors of Howth Castle would always be open to anyone seeking food and shelter."

"I heard that story, but how...?"

"I'm getting to that. After his return, he was a figure of ridicule to his peers. His father disowned him and moved the family back to England. Mick never saw his family again."

"His family left him? It wasn't his fault, how could they? What did Mick do?" I sit up and stare at Niamh. I can't believe a family could be so cruel.

"Mick sought his revenge on Grace. He captured one of her ships and drank from a cask he thought to be wine. Instead, it was an elixir our Queen had found to strengthen her magic. We were afraid Mick would die. Instead, he became a powerful, immortal wizard."

"He has been without family for hundreds of years?" I blink to keep back the tears. "How lonely he must be with no family or friends."

"We are his friends, he has us. Now get ready, you have a ball to attend." I sit still as Niamh gathers things for me to wear.

I quietly ask, "Niamh, what does 'mo chuisle' mean?"

"My love. My heart."

Niamh leaves and I go into the adjoining bath chamber. I hope that a long hot shower will manage to steam away most of my brain fog and any lingering soreness. Now, if it could only wash away my embarrassment.

♣♣♣

I sit at the vanity table in my new gown, ready to attend the ball. Wish I wasn't a nervous wreck. Someone knocks on the door, "Come in."

Mick walks in as a dog. He jumps up on the vanity seat next to me, leans over, and drops a box in my lap. I stare at him in the mirror, then at the box.

"Another gift?"

"Please open it."

I look inside the beautiful gold box. There's a deep blue sapphire and diamond ring. "This is the most beautiful ring I've ever seen."

"Do you like it?"

"I love it. It's beautiful. This is way too much. I can't accept it."

"Please do not insult the giver by not accepting. It is a way of saying, you are loved."

I grab Mick and hug him. I rub my face in his fur, then remember and push him away.

"You aren't a dog. What are you doing?"

Mick stands and transforms into a man. He's wearing an elegant outfit that I've never seen in 'Vogue', black slacks and a white Spanish style short jacket that sets off his tan beautifully. I try so hard not to stare. He's gorgeous.

"I wanted to tell you so often. When I was teaching you not to be afraid of heights, I was close to breaking my word. I wanted to hold you as a man, to be there for you and comfort you as a man, not as a dog. I don't understand why your ancestors thought I might be a distraction."

I look at the puzzled look on Mick's handsome face and start laughing.

"Yup, you're a distraction. I understand their worry."

Mick looks at me as if I'm crazy and then starts laughing also. He sits down next to me.

"I don't get this distraction bit, but at least you don't despise me." He reaches over and holds my hand.

"How can I despise you? You are my friend, an important part of my life."

Mick gets this funny look on his face then drops down on one knee and takes my hand in his. Oh my gosh!

"Bridget Carins would you do me the honor of being my friend, long enough so that you get to know the real me and then I will replace this little token of our friendship with a real jewel to match your beauty."

"From you? A friendship ring? But you're a Lord."

Mick lifts me up from my seat and kisses me. Wow..., when I recover I realize that kiss is definitely a ten plus on the Richter scale!

I look at him. "Mick, I'll always be your friend, but I have a million questions before I can commit to anything else."

Another knock on the door and Molly walks in. She sees Mick on one knee and smiles. "I am so sorry to interrupt, but I thought you would like to know that Mary is now fully awake and wants to see you."

"That's great, thank you Molly." I jump up to hug her and almost knock Mick over. I go back and sit in front of Mick.

"Mick, I'll always be your friend, and I like the idea of getting to know each other more, but right now I hafta show this to Mary. She's going to go bananas."

"Bridget what questions do you have? We are meant to be together. I know you may need time. You have not had much time to get to know me...."

"That's not it. I know you Mick. All that I know is fantastic, even how dang stubborn you are. But, don't you see, I can't be more than friends with you."

"If it is our ages, I am less than a dozen years your senior."

"What, more like eight hundred years my senior."

"We age differently in the Fae world. Go now and I will explain later. Not to worry, we have many more years my love."

"How old are you?"

"My ageing stopped at age twenty five.

"Yeah but I'm just so... human. I'm nothing special, not compared with a faeire. They are the most beautiful people I've ever seen. They can live forever, and if we get serious, then when I age, you will remain the same, and I'll look like your mom."

"You have the blood of your ancestors. There will be a way for us. I will make it my quest to find one, but you must accompany me. I want you in my life. I have waited too long. I cannot leave you now and who knows what problems you will encounter on your own," he smiles and holds me close.

"I'll be your friend and go with you on your quest but first, I have to see Mary."

I jump up and walk towards the door. When I look back, Mick looks puzzled. I run back and hug him tight.

"I'll be right back." I run from the room before Mick reads the doubts and fears that keep surfacing.

I quietly knock on the door. Molly said that Mary is doing terrific, but I need to see for myself. Simon opens the door, comes out and hugs me.

"Bridget, how are you? We were crazy with worry until Molly came by to let us know you were resting. Mary will be happy to see you. I will leave her in your care and change for the ball, shall I?"

"That would be great. Are you sure she's okay? Does she remember much?"

"Nothing at all, the thrall that Dagda put her under was not harmful, but it would have been damaging if you hadn't rescued her when you did."

I open the door to see Mary sitting on a loveseat. She starts to jump up and run to me, but I beat her to it. We hug and cry, look at each other. Then hug and cry some more. Finally, exhausted we both sit on the yellow flowered loveseat and say at the same time, "How are you?"

We laugh and I ask, "You first, please tell me if you're okay?"

"I'm still so thirsty. I think I drank a dozen gallons of tea since I got here. Molly put me in this guest room to rest while she attended to some last minute details. Can you believe this place? Your family is incredible. No wonder you had a hard time telling me about them, I think I'd have a hard time describing them, and I've met them."

"Told ya." I laugh.

"I didn't want you to get caught up in the middle of this war. That is why I didn't tell you too much about the training or about the castle or anything."

"Okay, tell me what's up. You have won the war, saved your family and their land and you don't look right. You should be dancing on clouds now, not looking in the dumps."

"Mick gave me a ring."

"The dog!"

"Oh yeah, the humans are the only ones, not in on the big joke. Hey, no wonder Ms. Bunny was so down on men. She knew all along that Mick was human, well sort of, well not a dog anyway, and that he was lying to me."

I look at the puzzled look on Mary's face and explain, "Guess what, I can talk to the animals. Not just Mick in dog form, you can just call me Ms. Doolittle." I laugh.

"Sounds as though we have a lot of catching up to do," Mays says. "So Mick the dog is human?"

"Mick is a human that's a handsome wizard. He's hundreds of years old, but he ages well, he doesn't even look over twenty-five." I try to smile, but fail miserably.

"He gave me this," I show Mary my hand. "As a friendship ring until we get to know each other better." I can't help it. I sob on Mary's shoulder.

"Wow kiddo, not only a King, Queen, and castle but now you even have a Merlin in your life. How could anyone be so lucky?"

"Lucky? Don't you see? He's handsome, and I'm...well, me?"

"You nut, have you looked in the mirror today? You're beautiful. You've always been beautiful but with all the fresh air, exercise and nutritious food, you look like you could be on the cover of 'Vogue'. That's if they would ever have someone on there with boobs."

She accomplished what she planned to do. I burst out laughing and knuckle punch her on the shoulder. "Hey, I do look fabulous don't I?" I jump up and show off my new gown.

Mary has been given a gown in various shades of green. Set off by gold and emerald jewelry, she looks fantastic.

"You don't look like a slotz yourself." We laugh at old Mrs. Slotnick's Yiddish word.

I sit back down, "I don't know Mary. I love Mick, but I'm worried."

"What does he want to do?"

"He wants to go on a quest, to find a way to make me immortal like him."

"What about finding a way to make him mortal like you?"

"I don't know if he can. He's old now. If he becomes mortal, does he turn to dust? I couldn't take that chance. I do love him, and I guess I'm being a little dramatic about it all. So you have a boyfriend that's a spy, and I have one that can shift to a dog. Hey, so what's not to love?" I laugh.

"You better not go questing until after the wedding!"

"Wedding?"

"Yeah girlfriend, who else will help me pick out everything?"

She holds up her hand and shows me the beautiful diamond engagement ring, I didn't even notice before. I hug her tight, and we both cry again. I know we are both thinking of her mom and how much she wanted Mary to be happy and settle down.

I hold a crying Mary when I feel snowflakes on my face. I look up and see a woman. She has her arms around a handsome man and they are both smiling at us. I'm looking at Mr. and Mrs. Gallagher but I can't hear them. "Uh, Mary, turn around and tell me if you see anything?"

"What?"

Mary turns around and sees her mother and father smiling at her. She stares at them as if listening and after a few minutes they fade away. I suppress a sob but can't seem to stop the tears.

"Mary, are you okay?"

"I'm great. You know what they said?"

"No, I didn't hear anything."

"Mom wants you to know how much she loves you and misses your shenanigans." We laugh. "She and dad are extremely happy for me. They can't visit me again, but they will be watching over both of us always."

We both cry again until we hear a soft bell sound announcing the opening of the ball. We rush to fix our make-up.

The commons have been transformed to a ball with hundreds of Fae gathered. Some Fae dance in the grass, others dance in the air. I look at a kaleidoscope of color. Rainbow hues with vivid sparkling greens, pinks, yellows, all bright multicolored flashes abound, as more faeire arrive with their brilliant wings spread.

I see Molly dancing in the air with Evelyn screaming with delight as her mother holds her and they dance among the treetops.

Fergus comes over and bows. "You look decidedly lovely my dear. It was a blessing meeting you." With that said, he walks directly to the great, large white oak in the center of the commons, and disappears.

Peter is dancing with Michelle. She's wearing an incredible creation that I must see up close, but not now, she's so happy, she glows almost as bright as the garland of flowers she wears in her hair.

Que-tip is dancing and flirting outrageously with the Selkie I met on the ferry.

Mary is sitting with a bedazzled Simon. Next to them, on a raised platform are King Padraig and Queen

Geraldine. The Queen is no longer transparent. She looks whole and healthy.

I continue to look around in awe. "It's hard to believe that this was a battlefield last night."

Padraig and Geraldine appear next to where Mick and I stand. "You look wonderful mo chuisle." My perfectly formed Great says. I reach out and hug her tightly for the first time. I look at her and Padraig and feel so loved.

"Thank you both for everything." I twirl around to show them the dress and shoes.

Padraig smiles, "Our pleasure my dear, we all have so much to thank you for. Ah, what a beautiful ring, looks like a Howth heirloom if I am not mistaken."

I hold out my ring. "It is a friendship ring from Mick. I turn to Mick, "Why didn't you say something about the ring being part of the Howth jewels? Holy smoke, I can't take anything so valuable?"

"I waited a long time for someone worthy to wear it."

I look at the ring and then Mick. If I leave Mick, I'll have an aching sense of loss that will never go away. Mick is a part of me now. I resolve not to worry about tomorrow and live for today. Then and there I decide to keep the ring and keep Mick in my life forever.

I explain, "It is a friendship ring. We are going to spend some time getting to know each other. Oh wait, I will need to go back to Brooklyn. Traveling will be expensive, and I have to get a job and...."

The Greats and Mick laugh. "There you go again, are you worrying about money?" Mick grins.

Molly fly's over. "Dear I have my own little gift of thanks for you. You liked my little apartment in Dublin. I own it, and now it is yours. She looks at the Great's. I won't be needing it much, but I may stop by now and then for a visit."

"Of course as our only living direct descendant you do own the lands in Ireland and Scotland and several other little spots around the world," says Geraldine.

"My dear, you are a billionaire many times over. You never have to work again if you don't wish to," says Padraig right before he catches me. I think people really do faint in real life.

I come to in Mick's arms, "My real life Prince Charming!" He takes my hand, bows and kisses it. Padraig and Geraldine look pleased. I blush and look around.

"I can't believe this is the same place."

"Now you can see what a happy people we are."

"'What did you do with you know who?"

"We thought she might enjoy the view in the donkey shed."

We all laugh with Padraig. Tristan, Que-tip, Shennum and Niamh join us.

I turn to Queen Geraldine and ask, "What now?"

"It is up to all of us. We must reverse the evil that has been done. First we celebrate." With a wave of her hand, we all join the dancers.

The stature of Morrigan is in a small, dark, donkey shed. The shed door opens, and two giant Newts enter. They look at the statue of the Goddess captured in stone with a shocked expression on her face. They pick up the statue and leave. They walk across the land and go deep in the woods to a small lake. They enter the water taking the statue of Morrigan the Goddess of War with them.

Some of you may have questions, if so please turn the page for the Author's Ramblings

Almost thirty years ago, a retired logger told me the most important thing to remember about living in the Northwest is to *"Plan to wear out and not rust out."* So when I became a great-grandmother I realized that there are a few things I have dreamt of doing that I haven't done yet. That included writing a novel.

♣

I have been asked many questions about writing a novel and hope to answer a few questions here.

If you have a question, please be sure to email me at, bcrepeau4551@comcast.net   I would love to hear from you.

Why did you decide to write?
Long story that I like to tell but for those people who do not wish to read that much of my ramblings, let's just say, prayer and dreams.

Any intriguing things happen while you were writing?
If by, intriguing you mean, woo-woo. Then yes it did. In book two, Bridget, my protagonist, speaks with vets from World War II and fresh home from the Stan or Afghanistan.

When I was typing on automatic, *(like automatic writing except you use a keyboard),* I kept typing the name, Florence Nightingale. Now Flo was from the Crimean War, not the right time frame at all. Three times I had to backspace and delete her name.

I went on-line to see if I could find out more about St. Paul's Cathedral, for example, where my villains could plant bombs for the most damage possible.

Side note: I really am a nice person but my friends at the Portland Police Bureau think I made it to the 'Homeland Security' list with book one, when I went on-line to find what would be found in a terrorist stockpile. Luckily they don't know I was virtually casing St. Paul's for bomb sites. At least I don't think they know...☺

Anyhow, back to my on-line research for St. Paul's. I found a tourist handout that described Wellington's tomb in the "crypt below the Cathedral." Wow, perfect. What better place for a bomb then a crypt? Now, where in the crypt? Reading many more pages a name popped up... you guessed it. Florence Nightingale is buried in the crypt below St. Paul's.

Another woo-woo thing I discovered was while I was writing book three, Magical Scotland. I wanted to tie up any lose ends. To let you know that Mary and Simon are getting married, as well as Peter and Michelle, and probably Mick and Bridget, if she finds he is as charming in human form as he was as a dog. ☺

In looking for more loose ends, I realized I mentioned the reason the negative publicity about France was to have them lose out on their bid to be the next site for the Olympics. I mentioned that someone from the United States must have been the culprit who masterminded the dog napping and media mess so that the US could move up the line and be picked for the next Olympic site.

> **Side Note:** *Since my days working in Protective Services, Community Policing and Domestic Violence Intervention,* I don't watch the news or read the newspapers. I figure that if anything happens that I need to know, *(even if I don't want to know it)* someone will love to tell me all the gory details of buy-outs, murders, etc. No one tells me the nice stuff. Like the next Olympic site.

I wondered what happens to the people when it is decided that they need to leave their homes, so a stadium can be built. The numbers of dislocated people made my story about Bridget's neighbors being dislocated very real, and then... I read...Paris, France misses being the next site of the Summer Olympics. That gave me goose bumps for sure.

Will you be writing more Brooklyn Leprechaun mysteries?
Not right away, Helen may start some shenanigans in Italy, we will see.

I have actually written a Screenplay entitled, The **Brooklyn Leprechaun!** My screenplay; (I describe as Pirates *of the Caribbean meet Alice in Wonderland,)* will be sent to agents, contest, etc. Unfortunately marketing is not as much fun as writing.

Hopefully some day you may be able to bring your great grandchild to the theater and say.... Hey, I remember that book!

The final question that I am asked is why I dedicated my first book to the Head Start program.

I always look for ways to give back to the Head Start program. Head Start convinced me that I could do anything. I joined as a victim and left as a leader.

> **Side Note:** Since 1965, more than 27 million low income children and their parents have benefited from Head Start.
> Graduates have gone on to be Members of Congress, the US Treasurer, award-winning athletes, poets, and musicians.

Thank you so much for reading my books. I hope that they entertained and inspired.

Wishing you the very best!

Bernadette W. Crepeau

Made in the USA
Charleston, SC
05 March 2012